His Father's Sins

By Kellye Bel Davis Alston

This novel is a work of fiction. Names, characters, places, and incidents either are the product of the author's imagination or are used fictitiously, and any resemblance to actual persons, living or dead, businesses, companies, events, or locales is entirely coincidental.

Library of Congress Cataloging-in-Publication Data
His Father's Sins/ Kellye Bel Davis Alston
ISBN 978-0-9854894-4-1
Front and Back Cover Design by The Intelligent Consulting Design Team

www.intelligentpublishing.org

Acknowledgements

I would like to thank my sweet, Holy Father for the gifts and talents, the passion and the desires that were developed in order for this book to get to this point. I am so filled with gratitude that He loves me enough to grant my request of becoming an author. I have a burning desire for this dream to unfold and touch every reader that flips through the pages. I do now believe that I can do all things through Christ who strengthens me. Again to God, I humbly give thanks.

I thank my husband, Patrick Alston, who is my soul mate and my number one fan. You will never know what your support has meant throughout our two decades plus. It's your gentle spirit, yet your strength and love for me, our children and for God that makes me feel that I can fly. I love you and thank you for being such a man about it.

I thank my family, my Mama and Daddy for being supportive through everything I've ever done and reading my dramas, even when you might not feel like it. You are the best parents ever and I know my love for life is a direct reflection of the love you've always shown; thanks to my mother-in-law for being with me from the beginning of this dream to write, always reading, encouraging and cheering me on. You and Dad are also the best parents-in-law ever.

Thanks to my four beautiful daughters, Taylor, Kennedy, Chandler and Logan. I love you girls more than life and I am so proud of you all. Each of you has a way of inspiring me to do great things. I hope to inspire you as well.

Thanks to the wonderful and genuine female relatives and friends who read as I wrote: Lois Davis, Beverly and Taylor Alston, Leontyne Scott, Kathy Pittman, Vanessa Brown, Katina Chism, Jimmi Lampley, Shelby Thomas, Tonya Duncan, Marilyn Anderson, Yvonne Carr, Hazel Burks, and Kimberly Ward for boosting my confidence all of the way. You have no idea how much it mattered. You ladies are awesome.

Thanks to Intelligent Consulting Company with Wendy Peterson for taking on a new project, for believing in it and working so diligently to make it happen in a timely manner.

Thanks to each reader that opens this book and any others that I write. I pray that my stories will always lift your spirits and entertain your souls. To God be the glory!!! I LOVE YOU ALL!

Chapter 1

"This will be the best Thanksgiving ever, baby. It'll be your first time meeting everybody. I can't wait for my brother to meet you. He's going to love you," LaQuincy said as he picked up his wife's last piece of luggage to put in the cab.

"You really think so?" Diara responded nervously.

"Oh yeah, everyone will," he reassured her and said, "He's been gone now for two years.

I never thought I'd say it, but I miss him more than I thought I would."

"He's very important to you, isn't he?" Diara asked.

"Sure he is," LaQuincy answered.

"He's my big brother. We've been through a lot together. We haven't always gotten along, but for the most part, that guy is my hero. Hey Man," he yelled to the cab driver. "Can you step on it? We don't want to miss our flight. I got to take this beautiful lady home to meet Moms and the Fam."

Diara smiled and sank into LaQuincy's arms, kissing him passionately. "I wish you had done this last night, but when you turn your back to me, I know what that means," said LaQuincy, " and maybe it's my imagination, but it's getting to be a habit."

Diara quickly replied, "No honey, I've just not been feeling great lately. I want you to have me when I'm at my best."

"But I'm your husband, and to me, you're always at your best," said LaQuincy.

"Shhh, Come here," said Diara, kissing him as the driver rushed through traffic to get to the airport while stealing peeks of the couple through his rearview mirror.

LaQuincy caught him and winked back at him, causing him to quickly place his eyes on the road and focus on the destination.

An attendant from the baggage department quickly grabbed the bags as the cab door opened. LaQuincy paid the driver and grabbed his bride's hand to help her out of the car.

Diara smiling brightly, said, "You are such a gentleman. Will you always be this good to me?"

"No doubt baby, as long as you don't change," he replied.

"You mean the world to me, girl."

After the flight attendant gave final instructions for boarders to feel free to release their seatbelts, another attendant brought the cart by to see who wanted drinks.

"I'll have a coke please," said LaQuincy.

"I'll have the same," said Diara.

"Hey baby, you don't have to avoid drinking because I can't have one. It's my problem, not yours. I have been alcohol free for over a year now. It becomes less and less of a problem for me every day. However, it has nothing to do with you. I know how you enjoy your wine and it might help you relax. You seemed a bit nervous when we boarded. Give her a glass of that Sutter Home Chardonnay please. Are you afraid to fly?" asked LaQuincy.

"Terrified; always have been," answered Diara. "As much traveling as I do, no one would ever believe it. It's not so bad if I have someone to talk to, but I never fly alone," she said. "If no one can travel with me, I drive or postpone the shoot, meeting, or whatever," said Diara.

"Wow, girl you got it bad don't you?" Replied LaQuincy.

"Yea, but I'll be okay," says Diara, trying to convince herself. "I have you and since you insist, I'll have a glass of wine, but if I'm tipsy, I warn you. I might embarrass you in front of your family."

"You could never embarrass me baby. You are much too pretty for that. And as long as I'm around, you will never fly alone," said LaQuincy as he took the cup of wine from the attendant's hand, gently passing it to Diara. "Enjoy this wine Boo. I'm cool."

"Okay," said Diara as she pulled the glass to her lips.

When they arrived, at least ten of the family members ran out of the house to meet them. LaQuincy began to introduce them one by one.

"So this is the beautiful Diara, huh," said LaQuincy's father, Sam.

His sister Jackie joined in, agreeing with Sam, "Boy how did you find somebody that pretty? She must be blind, cripple and crazy." Everyone hugged, laughed, and walked into the house. After putting away their luggage, Diara settled into their weekend living quarters, while LaQuincy followed his nose to the kitchen where he knew he would find his mother.

"Son, you look so happy, and Diara is simply gorgeous," said Dee.

"Thanks Ma, she is beautiful isn't she? She is just awesome in every way. I never met anyone quite like her. She makes me feel like I can do anything."

"Oh that is so wonderful," said Dee, teary eyed. I am so happy for you Quin. You have been through so much. God is smiling on you baby. You need to thank Him. He pulled your feet out of the miry clay. You have this fabulous job now as a freelance photographer; working for K magazine, Ebony, Essence. Boy, your mama is so proud of you. I tell my friends, I don't know where my son Quin's going from one week to the next because he's in and out of the country all the time. Now you're married to this supermodel. I know you said she was a model, but which magazine were you shooting when you met her?"

Diara entered the kitchen at that moment, and LaQuincy grabbed her hand.

"She can tell you all about it Ma. I'm going to leave you ladies to talk and go holler at the old man." He kissed Dee on the cheek and Diara on the forehead as he turned to leave the room.

"Ok, baby," said Dee, "I know he's waiting for you.

Hi sweetie, come on in. Are you hungry?" she asked Diara.

"Hey Dad, what time is my knuckle head brother suppose to be here?" Asked LaQuincy.

"Oh he's not due in until 11pm," replied Sam.

"He always did like to make a grand entrance," laughed LaQuincy. "So Pops, how's Ma's health? I hope she's doing what she needs to do, having diabetes. It's nothing to play with."

"She's doing ok," said Sam. "She's not used to following orders, so you know how stubborn she can be, still trying to prove she's superwoman around here, but for the most part, she's hanging in there. What about you, Son? How's the married life?"

"Aw Dad," answered LaQuincy like a child with a new toy, "Diara is the woman of my dreams. She's smart, thoughtful, and sexy."

"She is that," stated Sam. "I wish we could've come to the wedding. I always thought I'd be there when my sons took their brides."

"Yeah, I know Dad, but it was all so sudden. It took a lot of convincing to make this woman marry me, so we just decided not to bother anyone with all the planning and everything that goes into a wedding," said LaQuincy.

"You just couldn't wait to marry that pretty little thing in there, could you?" Said Sam.

"Exactly," said LaQuincy.

"I got to say, I don't blame you, I would've begged too, " said Sam.

The two of them laughed as Sam patted his son on the back.Meanwhile, most of the women, LaQuincy's sisters, Jackie and Krissy, his mother, and a couple of cousins were in the kitchen, laughing and talking loud. Diara had excused herself to go to the ladies' room, feeling somewhat unsure of how she fit in with the family, when the kitchen door opened and in walked Rudy, dressed as the officer he was, an airman of the United States Air Force, wearing a three-button, dark blue coat, a crisp, sharply starched light blue shirt beneath it, and silver bars on his coat that symbolized his rank as First Lieutenant. Exciting yells filled the room as Rudy hugged the ladies in his family, whom he had not seen for two years. He lived in Panama, but had been stationed in Iraq for the last eight months. While he hugged his mother tightly, Diara walked into the kitchen. Immediately, Rudy released Dee, stood stiffly in his tracks, as if someone had ordered him not to move and asked, "Who is the most beautiful lady I've ever seen in my life?"

"She's your brother's wife dumb dumb," said Krissy.

"Yes, off limits big brother," said Jackie, "forbidden fruit."

"Well, hello there, Sis. I'm Rudy."

"Hi Rudy," she said and thought, "Oh my God! I'm Diara," she said smiling.

"My, I didn't know my brother had such good taste," Rudy stated while kissing her hand.

"Wow, with hands as soft as cotton." Diara blushed and Rudy stared into her eyes as if he'd just heard that he was sentenced for life.

"I see you met my wife, Big Bro," LaQuincy said as he approached Rudy from behind, breaking the spell Rudy appeared to be under. Rudy suddenly turned around to a greeting from LaQuincy with a tight and forceful hug. "Well look at you, Mr. Officer. Are you a gentleman?" LaQuincy asked as he turned to his wife.

"So what do you think of my big brother here Diara? He's the brains of the family."

Before Diara could answer, the fellows had their arms around each other walking slowly in the direction of their dad who was anxiously waiting to see his eldest son.

Thanksgiving weekend was a blast at the Carpenter home. Diara had enjoyed meeting everyone andhad been welcomed into the family with open arms. Dinner was wonderful. Dee had done most of the cooking with some help from each of the other ladies. She'd worked tirelessly to ensure that each of her sons had their favorite dish on the table. LaQuincy's was peach cobbler. He had always bragged to everyone about Dee's peach cobbler. According to him, his mama's peach cobbler was so good; it would make you slap your mama. Rudy's favorite dish was lasagna. It wasn't exactly traditional for Thanksgiving, but Dee wanted to make her boys happy. She missed cooking for them.

The last two days were upon them. Thanksgiving Day was now a blur. LaQuincy received a phone call Friday morning from Lawrence Dubois of America's Top Model, at Tyler Banks' request, stating that the photographer had taken ill on Thanksgiving night at home in Virginia and couldn't make it back to Los Angeles. They needed a photographer like yesterday, as DuBois put it. Kennedy Wane had given LaQuincy's name to Tyler and she wanted him ASAP. As much as he hated to cut his trip short, he knew he couldn't turn down an opportunity like this. He hoped they would like his work so well that he would become their permanent photographer. LaQuincy didn't know how to break the news to Diara that he had to leave in five hours. There wasn't enough time to fly back home to Chicago with her and he knew it would be Sunday night or Monday morning before he could make it back there.

Diara was in the living room enjoying a cup of coffee and reading the newspaper when LaQuincy told her the great news. She was so excited for him; she nearly leaped around his neck. Surprisingly, she handled the news well about him leaving earlier. In fact, she decided to rent a car and drive back home alone. LaQuincy thought that was a terrible idea. Rudy walked into the room and heard the couple discussing the issue. He quickly suggested a solution.

"I'm on leave for 30 days before I have to report back to Panama," said Rudy.

"Why don't I fly back to Chicago with Diara? I did hear you say she was afraid to fly alone right? Plus you already have tickets, so why let them go to waste? It's too far to drive. I don't know about you but I can't handle sixteen hours in a car. I'll fly there, get a hotel and head back the next day. Does that sound like a plan Diara?" said Rudy.

"Sure, I guess," she said softly, "if it's okay with you LaQuincy."

"Hey," said LaQuincy, "I love the idea. My baby doesn't have to fly by herself. We don't have to waste good tickets and what better hands could she be in other than my big brother's? Well, why don't the two of you drop me off at the airport? You can get to know each other better then."

Diara didn't seem too comfortable with the idea, but LaQuincy insisted.

"Come on baby," he begged. "I admit my brother is not the best driver in the world, so you might want to do the driving," he said, handing Diara the keys.

"No," she said smiling, giving the keys to Rudy.

"No, he's right," said Rudy, laughing as he gently pushed the keys back to Diara.

"I am chauffeured everywhere I go, on the ground and in the air," joked Rudy.

"You're an airman, man," said LaQuincy. "How do you get away with that?"

"I'm the medicine man," replied Rudy. "In another year, you can call me Dr. Carpenter."

"Man, that's awesome," said LaQuincy, hugging Rudy. "Baby, I told you he was the brains of the family. When we were kids, he was the only one that took playing doctor with the girls seriously. He would actually check their pulse." They all laughed. "The girls didn't even understand," LaQuincy continued. "They knew the idea of the game until they met Dr.R.C. here, who changed all of the rules."

Interrupting LaQuincy, Rudy said, "Man, you're pretty big time yourself, doing photo shoots for America's Top Model, and Ma tells me you're contracted by K Magazine, working for Kennedy Wane. Sounds like you're at the top of your game, boy!"

"It's this woman," says LaQuincy, grabbing Diara by her waist. "She's the best thing that ever happened to me. She's got me doing things I never thought I'd do."

"Oh, baby you give me too much credit. You're great at what you do," said Diara turning toward Rudy. "I've never seen anyone with so much passion about his work. He's been waiting for a call from America's Top Model for quite some time now. Once they see his work, he'll get the contract, because he's the best photographer out here. He's an artist behind a lens. They love him at K. Don't they Honey?"

They kissed. Rudy looked away and said, "Hey that's cool. I'm proud of my little brother. Like they say, behind every great man, there's an even greater woman. You're a lucky man, my brother," said Rudy, staring at Diara, raising his coffee cup.

LaQuincy and Diara looked at each other and smiled LaQuincy put his arm around her waist and they all walked into the kitchen for breakfast with the rest of the family. Dee is saddened by the news of LaQuincy leaving early, but reassured him that she was very proud of him.

"So what time does your flight leave Quin? Sam asked.

"I leave at 12:55. Therefore, I need to get my things together and get ready to head to the airport. Diara and Rudy are giving me a ride to the airport and Rudy's going to accompany my beautiful bride back home on her flight," explained LaQuincy.

Jackie whispered to Krissy, "I don't know if that's a good idea."

"Oh girl, please. They're brothers," says Krissy, annoyed by the thought.

"Umph! Maybe you didn't see the way Rudy looked at his sister-in-law when he got here," mumbles Jackie, receiving a dirty look from Krissy.

"Well fam, it's been real as always," announced LaQuincy, hugging his Dad, who stood up to say goodbye. "I'm going to get ready to hit the road. I need to make a couple of calls as well. Excuse me for a moment."

When LaQuincy returned to the dining room, Diara helped Dee clear the dishes. He headed straight to hug his mother, who tightly embraced him, as if it would be the last time they would see each other. He felt the dampness of her tears on his skin through his shirt. Diara saw how much love Dee felt for her son. It was almost painful to watch. She vaguely remembered experiencing love like this. It seemed like a lifetime ago. Her mother had died from a 3-year battle with cancer when Diara was only 12. Her father died a couple of years later in an alcohol induced car accident. He had become a reckless drunk after the death of her mother.

She recalled the depth of her parents' love. Her dad always spoke of her mom as the love of his life. He didn't deal well with her illness and certainly not her death. He drowned his sorrows in alcohol. After he died, she moved in with his half sister, the closest living relative, a coldhearted woman who took Diara in for a paycheck. The next four years were a living hell. The aunt constantly let Diara know that she was not really wanted there and as soon as the money ran out, she had to leave. After Diara's 18th birthday in February, the checks stopped and Diara was physically ejected into the street because Aunt Loody had received a letter noting the end of her additional income. She needed Jack Daniels and if Diara couldn't pay for it that day, she was out of there. Her heart ached as she pulled herself out of the dreadful memory and watched LaQuincy promise to visit his mother more often. How she longed for her mother, and her father.

"Ma, I'll call you when I get there, okay? And I'll come back as soon as I can," promised LaQuincy.

"I know baby. Forgive me for being so selfish," said Dee. "It's a Mama thing. You can't understand until you have children of your own."

"I'll miss you too Ma!" said LaQuincy. They hugged one last time and LaQuincy passed Diara on his way to the car, hoping she and his mother wouldn't notice the tears in his eyes.

Chapter 2

Sam dropped Rudy and Diara off at the airport. They hadto be there by 3:00 p.m. As they boarded the plane, one of the passengers said,

"Sir, your wife dropped her scarf. Rudy picked it up, said thank you to the man and didn't bother to correct him. Diara kept walking as if she was unaware of the incident. After being seated, Rudy ordered a glass of Chardonnay and a crown and sprite.

"Who told you I drank Chardonnay?" asked Diara.

"No one. You look like you could use a drink, and furthermore, a lot of classy ladies like white wine," explained Rudy.

Diara took a sip and put down the cup. "So, was I right?" asked Rudy.

"I guess," she said smiling sheepishly. They pushed back into their seats and relaxed as they flew quietly across the friendly skies.

"Are you always this quiet?" Rudy asked after chugging down the last swallow in his glass.

"Well no," Diara quickly replied. "I just figured you might want to relax."

"Please prepare for landing," the flight attendant said. "All passengers must fasten their seatbelts." Rudy and Diara listened carefully for their flight information. They weren't sure how long they would be laid over in Atlanta.

"Oh, we'll only be here for about 40 minutes, just long enough to get to our gate," said Rudy. "I have a friend in Atlanta that I would love to see, but maybe I can catch him on my way back through," Rudy said regretfully. "He and I started in boot camp together and stayed together for over 5 years. He went home with me once because his parents were going out of town for Christmas. My parents took him in and he enjoyed Christmas like the rest of the family. He's gone back there even when I couldn't make it home. He and Quin got pretty tight too. Now he's stationed in Atlanta, married and has a newborn baby boy. We keep in touch, though."

"Did he know you would be back to the states for the holiday?" Diara asked.

"Yes, he knew I would be home for Thanksgiving, but neither of us knew I would be coming through Atlanta,: he said and paused before continuing to say with almost laughter, "Cross is a comedian. He kept everybody in good spirits even when you wanted to cry."

As Diara looked out of the window nervously, she announced, "Oh boy, here comes that dreadful landing."

Before Rudy could respond, the wheels had hit the runway with a hard thump. When Rudy looked at Diara, her eyes were closed tightly and hands stretched forward. As if it were a natural reaction, Rudy took hold of Diara's hand and placed it in his hand. She squeezed his hand hard until the aircraft came to a complete stop. Diara couldn't help but laugh as she opened her eyes and realized that her brother-in-law had allowed her to use him in her panic.

"Did I hurt you?" she asked, releasing his hand. "Quincy does that for me. It's funny that I never know what I'm squeezing until the plane stops. That's been rather awkward sometimes in the past." She said with a bit of laughter. "I once opened my eyes and was holding a man's toupee'. I guess I'd snatched it right off his head. Needless to say, he wasn't very happy." They laughed as Rudy retrieved Diara's bags from the overhead compartment.

When the two of them reached their gate, they learned that the flight would be delayed for another hour. Rudy called his friend Terrance Cross while Diara placed her bags in a chair, preparing to stay for a while.

"Well, are you hungry?" Rudy asked.

"Cross said he would get here as soon as he could, but I'm sure he'll text me and I'll let him know where we are. I see a couple of decent looking restaurants, not far from our gate. I could use a steak myself."

"I guess I could eat something. A steak does sound good," said Diara. "Oh, there's a ladies' room. I'll be right back. Could you watch my bags please?"

"Sure," said Rudy. He also watched Diara's slender body as she walked away. She wore a fitted, rust colored, vneck sweater that dipped to the entrance of a size 36 cleavage. Her snug fitting, size 10 Levi boot cut jeans did her curves justice. He thought she was just perfect, from her naturally curly locks to her worn, rust colored, suede cowboy boots. Shaking his head he thought, "I'm still convinced my brother has married the most beautiful woman I've ever seen. Umph, stop it Rudy!" He warned himself. When Diara returned, they each grabbed a bag, and then Rudy took a bag from Diara, leaving her with just her purse to carry.

"Wow, your mom knew how to raise her sons. You and my husband are such gentlemen." complimented Diara.

"Thanks." said Rudy. "I'll be sure and tell her you said that. Here's a cozy little spot that probably has steaks." The restaurant was small, but elegant; with velvet mustard colored high back chairs, beige and brown, marble top tables with a lighted candle in a red glass holder as its centerpiece. The lighting was dimmed purposely, as if the room demanded the company of lovers only. Along the walls were small booths made for two.

"It's a little too cozy; and crowded, except for the one booth over there and that's just a little too intimate, don't you think?" said Diara.

"Would you like to go somewhere else?" asked Rudy, placing the menu he'd been admiring, back on the podium. "We can find another place if you're worried about seating, but there is a 10 oz rib eye steak on this menu," he said holding up the menu up next to his exaggerated smile, "with my name on it," hoping to persuade.

"Ok ok, we can stay," she said, finally agreeing.

Instantly, a hostess appeared, asking for the number in their party and then escorting them to the booth in question. A waiter came right away to give details about the day's specials and to take their drink orders. Rudy ordered a bottle of wine.

"So, you enjoy a glass of wine now and then yourself as well, humph," Diara commented.

"Sure, in fact, I'm very fond of the grape," answered Rudy laughing. "I would say I'm a connoisseur. I prefer dry wines, red and white. I choose my wine according to the food I'm having," he said.

"That's very interesting," said Diara, surprised that he would be so detailed when it comes to wine.

"What's interesting?" asked Rudy. "Well, that you put so much thought into it. I just enjoy a glass of wine and think nothing of it," she said. "Well, I've been accused all my life of overanalyzing things," Rudy replied. "Whatever I enjoy, I tend to give it very special attention. I become very focused and I study it because I want to know every detail about it. What makes it what it is? Is it even as great as I thought it might be? Is it worth my time?" He went on.

"Are we still talking about wine?" Diara questioned with laughter.

Interrupted by the waiter, "Can I take your order please?"

Rudy says, laughing as well. "I'm still deciding. I know I want the 10 oz rib eye, medium well, but I'm undecided on the veggies. Maybe the lady knows what she wants."

"Yes I do," Diara says without hesitation. "I'll start with a spinach salad with vinaigrette dressing. Then I'll have the 4oz filet mignon, medium," she continued, still scanning the menu, "béarnaise sauce on the side, broccoli and new potatoes, and no dessert for me please."

"You do indeed know what you want. Very precise," complimented Rudy. "I'll have the same veggies as the lady and no dessert for me as well," he said, obviously impressed with Diara's choices.

"Great, I'll put your order in right away," the waiter said while refilling their wine glasses and picking up their menus.

"So, are you always so direct and straight forward?" asked Rudy.

"Yes, in every area of my life," answered Diara. "You know or you don't know. I've always heard; if you study long, you study wrong. And it just so happens that whenever I linger in decision making, I end up regretting the choices I make." Before long, Rudy and Diara were laughing and feeling as comfortable as any married couple. They cracked jokes about each other, gazed at each other romantically, especially when they heard Brown Eyed Girl from the Isley Brother's 3+3 album. They even shared their steaks with each other.

Rudy paid the waiter with a credit card.

"Hey, you didn't have to do that," said Diara.

"I wanted to," said Rudy. "You are great company. I can't remember the last time I felt so comfortable with someone, or laughed so loud. My brother is a lucky man, and I think he knows it."

"Thank you for saying so, but he's a great guy," Diara said. "I'm the lucky one," she added.

"So, are you in a relationship right now?" She asked.

"No," answers Rudy. "I'm flying solo right now. I have had the company of many beautiful women and I have been in relationships that were fulfilling. In fact, I just got out of a threeyear relationship with a wonderful woman. She said she was running out of time and she wanted to be married. I wasn't ready for that with her. To this day, I have only met one woman in all my life that I would marry at the drop of a dime, and she belongs to another man," said Rudy, staring at Diara in an effort to send a message.

Breaking the silence, a voice came over the loud speaker giving boarding information.

"Hey, that's us. It's time for us to board," says Diara. "We need to get moving."

Grabbing the bags, Rudy and Diara hurried to the gate, which was near the restaurant.

"RUDY," a voice called out. "Hey man, I know I'm too late."

It was Terrance Cross. "Call me later. That's a beauty you got there with you."

"Yea, I'll call you," Rudy yelled back. "This is my brother's wife."

"Wow, you did good boy," Terrance called out. "No, you got it…"

"Yea, he didn't hear you. Just call him later. We need to run," said Diara.

A flight attendant met them at the entrance of the plane.

"Do you mind if we ask you and your wife to move to first class," she asked Rudy. "We have some additional passengers that have joined us unexpectedly in an emergency situation. They…

" "No, we don't mind at all. Do we honey?" Diara asked Rudy.

"Well no. That's fine with me," said Rudy smiling joyfully.

They turned down food and drinks, the perks of flying first class, enjoyed more conversation for a short period of time, at least until Rudy dozed off. After awhile his head was on Diara's shoulder. She didn't object because his warm breath gave her body a tingling feeling that she tried to ignore and would never admit, yet she allowed him to stay. Rudy was awakened by the sweet smell of Diara's hair, and the smoothness of her skin on his cheek. Suddenly his mouth watered with the temptation of licking her breast, while his hands longed to spread her legs apart just to feel the heat he knew would meet them. He felt the bulge against his pants as he imagined Diara wanting everything he had to offer. She closed her eyes, choosing to act as though she had no part in what was taking place. Rudy breathed in deeper, and then exhaled, as if he was purposely blowing on her breast to see how they would react, but she knew he was asleep, so she was reading something into this that just wasn't there, yet her breast reacted, without permission. Rudy noticed. He thought his man shaft would jump right out of his pants and expose him to everyone in first class. The hardness of her nipples made Rudy realize that he was not alone. She wanted this or she would have removed his head when it first lay on her shoulder. He looked up at her, without fear of being rejected. She continued pretending to sleep, but her tongue betrayed her as it licked slowly across her bottom lip provoking her head to tilt, leaving her bare neck in view. He watched in hunger, like a lion watches its prey just before pouncing. Never had he seen a sight so beautiful and inviting. He wanted her right here and now, but the plane was landing. The attendant was asking the passengers to fasten their seatbelts. Diara's eyes opened wide during the announcement. She grabbed Rudy's hand and squeezed it, painfully killing the moment. In the cab, they laughed openly about Rudy's aching hand, but chose not to mention the open foreplay they had encountered prior to the plane landing.

Chapter 3

L.A. had proved to be everything LaQuincy thought it would be. Most of the models were photogenic and very cooperative, which made his job easier. Some of them were exceptionally beautiful, while LaQuincy quietly questioned how and why some of the girls hadeven been chosen. This was his second day on the job and he had already won over the entire Tyler Banks crew. They loved his work and complimented his way with the models, who seemed extremely comfortable with him. He would be heading back to the hotel soon. He looked forward to hearing his wife's sweet voice. He had only spoken with her once since he had arrived. He realized that she would be traveling most of the day today. Therefore, he decided to wait for her call. He missed her, everything about her. He wondered if she missed him as much. He also wondered if she had been alright on the plane, feeling that no one could make her feel as safe as he could. He could hardly wait to leave the following morning.

"That's a wrap," he gladly yelled. His job was done. He was out of there.

LaQuincy was just leaving the studio when Ron yelled for him. Ron was one of the producers for America's Top Model. He caught up with LaQuincy to deliver some news LaQuincy did not want.

"We will need you for at least two more days. I hope your schedule is clear, if not, clear it. It's not every day we get a photographer like you in here. Tyler is very impressed with your work; very impressed," he repeated. "You never know. This could be the start of something big. What can I say;" he said cheerfully, "the girl loves who she loves." Ron kept walking. After he was sure Ron was out of sight, LaQuincy yelled, "DAMMIT!"

When he finally got to his hotel room, he checked his cell phone. There was a text from Diara and three missed calls from her. He must have missed them while he was working. There is a no cell phone policy on the set, of course. Therefore, his phone couldn't even be set on vibrate. It had to be on silent.

Diara's message read, "Hi honey, I'm finally home; at least in a cab heading that way. I feel like I've been flying for three days already. Glad to be back. It was wonderful meeting your family. I think they're all great. Call me with your homecoming arrangements so I can pick u up. Love u, D."

He called right away and her phone went to voicemail. After a couple of tries, he called Rudy's phone that also went to voicemail. "Maybe they went to get dinner. She'll call back," he thought. LaQuincy ordered room service and hopped in the shower.

After dinner, LaQuincy tried calling both phones again with a repeat of the same from earlier. He began to get worried. He called his parents' house. His mother had heard from Rudy while he was in the cab to Diara's and LaQuincy's home. He told her that after he helped Diara get safely situated in the house, he would take the cab to a hotel near the airport and he'd be home the next day. LaQuincy somehow felt more at ease, knowing that his brother would be so concerned with his wife's safety. That was really cool of him. I owe him. She'd probably had such a tiring day on planes that she went to sleep early, he thought. After eating, he laid in bed, sent Diara a text that he wouldn't be back for at least a couple of days and finally drifted off to sleep watching an episode of MARTIN.

Chapter 4

"Make yourself at home," Diara said, while flicking on a light switch, causing a beautiful, blazing fire in the large fireplace and pushed a button that opened her custom made drapes to a picture window that spread as wide as the room. "I want to put my things away. I'll be right with you. Send the driver away," Diara said to Rudy, who was busy admiring LaQuincy's house.

He was in awe at the types of art his brother was sofond of. Diara had explained to him when they walked in that it was all LaQuincy's. He spent thousands of dollars on exotic art. That was his one true love. Otherwise, Diara was the interior decorator, and a fine one, Rudy thought. His brother's house was immaculate. The tall, cathedral ceilings beautified the bottom floor. The furniture was classical and rich, something one might find in an old Victorian home. The drapes were obviously custom- made, matching the texture of the furniture from room to room. The fireplace was made of white porcelain, on a pure white marble floor that was nearly covered by a polar bear bearskin rug. Rudy was impressed with his brother's fine taste.

"Wow, this place is beautiful," he said aloud, not realizing that Diara could hear him as she swayed down the winding staircase.

"Thank you," said Diara.

"Who knew my little brother would evolve in such a way," Rudy said gazing at the carvings on the high ceilings.

"So, you'll stay, right? I just received a text from Quincy. He won't be back for at least two more days. You see there's more than enough space. The guest room is ready," Diara said.

"I don't know if it's a good idea for me to stay, "Rudy stated in a low and sexy voice, as he headed for the door. "I really don't trust what I'm feeling here and I think it would be best for us all if I keep my plans. You heard me tell my mother that I would get a room near the airport and leave tomorrow." Diara followed him to the door.

"I really don't want to be alone. I have a great bottle of Chloe Dubois chilling in the fridge. I think we know what lines not to cross. I mean, we're adults here. What are you afraid of?" said Diara, trying to convince Rudy to stay.

"Where were you when we were flying first class? Was I alone, or were the signals I got from you in my dream?"

"Whatever do you mean?" She said, smirking playfully.

"Now I know I'd better go. You obviously don't know what you're saying," said Rudy, sure that he was making the best decision. "I enjoyed your company, though. I think you're a hell of a woman," he continued.

"Likewise," she said and they laughed, "I mean I enjoyed your company as well," said Diara.

They said goodbye. She slowly closed the door behind him, hoping that any second he would change his mind. When he didn't, she rushed to the window, pulled back the drapes and saw Rudy get into the cab.

"It's goodbye," she said, "and I know it's best."

After a couple of hours, Rudy called the house to let Diara know he made it to the room. He was staying at the Marriott Courtyard Hotel for the night, which was close to the airport, but he still hadn't made reservations for his trip back to Boston. When they hung up, Diara thought about their escapade on the plane. She felt such guilt, but at the same time, she desired the act that wouldn't have been optional had he stayed. She showered and tried watching television in bed. When that didn't work, she got out of bed, went downstairs, put on an apron and baked a sweet potato pie from sweet potatoes she had bought before Thanksgiving and didn't want them to go to waste. She'd finally thought of an excuse to call Rudy. When he answered, she could feel his smile through the phone.

"Would you like to sample some pie?" she asked.

"Are you kidding? I would love to sample your pie," he said chuckling. They both laughed out loud.

"I don't know what you think I said, but I just made a sweet potato pie and I wondered if you would like to try it."

"Sorry, I was just being bad," he said. "But no, as much as I would like some, I'm going to try to get out of here in the morning. It's too cold to get back into another cab, so I guess I have to pass."

"I didn't ask you to come over. I just asked if you wanted some pie," she said.

"Well yes, in that case, I would love some." Before she could shut the phone off, Diara quickly ran up the staircase, threw on some black opaque tights, a grey sweater dress that cut off mid thigh, and a pair of flat black suede boots. She then applied a light coat of foundation, eyeliner and mascara. On her way into the garage, she stopped to wrap the pie in Saran Wrap and headed to the Marriott Courtyard Hotel.

Rudy was waiting with a smile and a fresh pot of coffee. When he opened the door, he was pulling a shirt over his head. Diara could see how muscular he was.

Wow, that's beautiful. He did that on purpose, she thought, hoping her expression wouldn't show her excitement. They ate pie, drank coffee and talked for hours, as they had done the day before, while traveling. Rudy complimented her baking skills with every bite. When Diara looked at the clock, she couldn't believe where the time had gone. It was 2am. She felt that she needed to get home so he could be ready for his departure later. He promised to call her from the airport.

"Hey, thanks for the company and the pie. That was great," he said.

"Oh you're welcome. I was bored and when I'm bored, I bake, and I didn't want to eat alone. That could've been dangerous," explained Diara, smiling.

"Well, thanks for sharing," he said. "Okay, see ya," she said, hugging him. When Rudy hugged back, he hugged tightly and could smell her freshness. He kissed her neck.

"I am so sorry; I didn't mean to do that. That was a mistake," he said with much sincerity. Diara just smiled shyly.

"Hey, just call me when you get home and let me know you made it safely, alright?" He said.

"Will do," said Diara. And she did.

That's when they said their goodbyes. Afterwards, they both lay awake in beds on separate sides of a city, with lustful thoughts of one another.

The next day, Rudy checked out of the hotel just before noon and caught a cab to the airport. The next flight wasn't until6:50pm. Therefore, he called Diara's house, but after there was no answer, he caught a taxi, hoping she was home. Maybe they could hang out, have lunch or something until he got back to the airport. He had resolved in his mind that she was his brother's wife and he had to respect that.

When the taxi pulled in the circle driveway at Diara's house, Rudy got out of the car, ran up the three steps to the plantation style porch and rang the bell. He rang it again and again and then knocked, but got no answer. Finally, disappointed, he decided to give up; he walked back to the cab and got inside. Diara had been in the shower and had not heard the doorbell or the knocking, but as she came out of her bedroom, fully robed, she saw the cab leaving the circle driveway from the top of the stairs. She ran downstairs and opened the door in hopes that he would see her before going too far down the road. She thought he'd left much earlier, but she had to admit, she was glad he hadn't. She wanted to see him again before he left for Boston where his parents lived, but, unfortunately, it was too late, she thought.

He was gone. Disappointed, she closed the door and walked to the living room window. She hit a button that closed the drapes automatically, and tied the belt to her hot pink, terry cloth robe.

As she walked away from the window and toward the staircase, the doorbell rang. When Diara opened the door, she was pleasantly surprised to see that he'd come back. She hugged him instantly, and then was embarrassed about acting out so hastily. They stared into each other's eyes, both obviously fighting for restraint.

"Hey, I can't get a flight until six fifty this evening. I've already checked out of the hotel," he said.

"Oh please, by all means, get in here," she said, waving the cab driver away.

"You want to go to lunch?" He said. "Yes, or I can fix lunch here and take you to the airport later," she said.

"Cool," he agreed.

They talked while she prepared lunch. He even pitched in; cutting scallions for a special tomato based sauce Diara would pour over two baked boneless breasts of chicken.

"Excuse me," she said, "I just need to check these once more before I go upstairs to put on some clothes."

"Can I go?" He asked in a soft, deep and sexy voice.

"Excuse me," said Diara, surprised at his boldness.

"I'm sorry," he said, "I can't help myself. I want you. I can't ..."

"It's okay," she said, interrupting him. "I can't either. I want you. I wish that I didn't, but I do."

They began to kiss. She could feel him untying her robe. She shook from nervousness, but she knew once unrobed , her naked body would be exposed and she would not be able to stop the desires her body screamed for. After he opened her robe, he pushed her back gently. He wanted to see what he'd waited for so anxiously, feeling remorseful that the woman he loved on sight was his brother's wife, yet feeling that he was in too deep. It was too late to stop.

"I've never wanted anything as much as I want you," he whispered. How could you be made for me when you belong to another?" He continued. "I know you feel it too, don't you? I could see it in your eyes the first time we met."

Without resistance, Diara fell into Rudy's arms, crying. "Yes," she said softly. "I didn't want to feel it. I tried to fight it. I was content with him."

The robe dropped to the floor. He lifted her, kissed her naked body and her lips until they reached the bearskin rug in front of the fireplace.

"But are you happy with him?"

He gently wiped the tears that flowed freely from her eyes. He understood her guilt. He was closely related to the pain and regret she wrestled through as she began to moan from desire. She wondered momentarily if she really ever loved LaQuincy. And if she did, then how could she be overtaken in an instant by a stranger. Would LaQuincy understand matters of the heart and forgive her? Could he ever forgive his brother? She'd never felt like this before. Had she found the kind of love her father spoke of at her mother's funeral? She remembered him getting choked up as he tried to explain their kind of love. "It was the kind," he'd said, "that you feel down in your soul, the kind that even a little child could see." Is this that kind of love? Can it possibly happen this soon, in this way? She pondered.

Rudy was different. First of all, he was exceptionally handsome. His thick eyebrows looked as if they had been professionally drawn. He was 6 feet tall, caramel colored, with jet-black wavy hair. He smelled edible, she thought, as she tasted his smooth skin, while rubbing the rippling indentions of his chest with one hand and his wide, muscular back with the other. She felt safe; covered by his masculinity, engrossed in the pleasures his hands delivered to her hungry body. This feeling was heavenly, and new. Passion filled the air. Remorse was gone and love was there.

Rudy thought Diara was every man's dream. He ran his fingers through her hair and watched her like she would slip away and he would find himself dreaming. How someone could be so beautiful was a mystery to him. It was obvious that his brother had chosen her as carefully as he had chosen the beautiful pieces of art in his home, but was she just a trophy, or a piece of art to LaQuincy? Did he love her? Yes, he loved her, Rudy decided in his mind. How could he not? He hoped God would forgive him, for he had coveted another man's wife, and caused her to commit adultery.

He wondered if his brother would ever forgive and love him again, or if he would hunt him down to slay him. As he forced himself to escape wicked thoughts and tune back in to the picturesque Diara, they began to make love. Tears again flowed from Diara's eyes. No one had ever loved her body with such intensity. She could have sworn that his mission in life was to satisfy her every sexual need, ensuring multiple orgasms, 100% satisfaction. As they both reached a peak of explosion, Rudy held on to her as if his life depended on it, calling her name, shamelessly. "Diara" and she replied, saying, "I love you, Rudy," whispering in a sweet, soft voice.

The next couple of days felt surreal to both of them. Although, Diara talked and texted back and forth to LaQuincy, she and Rudy lived like man and wife in his brother's castle.

They dined by candlelight and slept in a guestroom that was nearly as lavish as the master bedroom. However, they made love all over the house, even in the kitchen, and they talked endlessly about life, their childhoods, and their dreams.

His heart went out to her when she lay in his arms sharing the story about her parents' deaths at her young and tender age. She had become vulnerable, looking for love in all the wrong places; one that would fill the void of having no parents. Nothing could, and nothing did, until now. She had always felt that a part of her had died with her mother, the part that was happy, loud and silly; the way she remembered herself as a child. She had shut down, but she could feel herself beginning to open like a beautiful sunflower. Rudy wanted to know everything about Diara, even down to the birthmark on the upper left part of her pelvis. They laughed at the story her mother had told her about it; that Diara was marked with money because she would be a wealthy woman someday.

In a few days, Rudy knew more about Diara than anyone. He had learned that she only appeared to be quiet and shy. She was actually very funny, intelligent and a beautiful person, inside and out. Her overbearing aunt had been loud and controlling. She had become accustomed to having no voice. However, with Rudy, she talked, laughed, and flirted nonstop. He knew things about her that no one else had ever even seemed to care about, not even LaQuincy.

She learned a lot about her husband's family as well, from Rudy. They had grown up with the love that Diara had witnessed over the Thanksgiving holiday, though they didn't have much money. However, his dad had been very controlling and demanding when the children were young, downright mean and selfish, according to Rudy, which caused problems for Rudy and his siblings as adults. His dad had been an alcoholic and had abused their mother for many years. Diara could hardly believe that such a mild mannered person could've ever been anything less than loving and kind, and she wondered how two such wonderful men like Rudy and LaQuincy could escape the inheritance of such temperament.

LaQuincy was kind. He would buy you the world if he could. He believed a woman should have the finer things in life. That's why his home was so extravagant. He wanted the beautiful Diara to bask in the glory of her surroundings, inside and out. On a walk, Diara showed Rudy the well kept grounds, the flower gardens and waterfalls, along with beautiful sculptures of all kind that gave the worldly appearance of someone who knew a lot about famous sculptures and statues of the world. That was important to LaQuincy. He liked to impress people. He loved hosting parties and events in his home. The couple attended celebrity dinner parties, Academy Awards and all other huge functions with the elite of Hollywood. They frequented the red carpets at different theaters in Cali. Celeb life with LaQuincy was busy and extraordinary. It had been a circle that Diara had strived for years to be a part of, which was what drew her to LaQuincy. He could get her there. Her self-worth centered on her outer beauty. Until now, no one had noticed that she had anything else to bring to the table.

Rudy, somewhat like LaQuincy, found Diara physically striking, exceptionally beautiful. However, he was an analytical thinker. It was the reason he was a high ranked officer in the air force, and the reason he was so intrigued by medicine. He was sharp, brilliant, and to Diara, that was the epitome of sexy. He interrogated like a lawyer, and was interested in every answer. For every answer, there was another question. Diara felt like she was talking to a therapist, as she disclosed any information that Rudy inquired about. Their conversations were like a spiritual renewal for her because never had she realized that she needed therapy until she received it with Rudy. She experienced purifying, cathartic moments with him. She laughed, she cried, she listened, and they'd make love again.

He was tender, caring, attentive and very romantic. The last evening before LaQuincy was due back home, Rudy drove Diara's black Cadillac CTS Sports coupe to a store nearby to buy fruit and chocolate syrup for chocolate dipped strawberries and grapes with wine. They fed each other later on the rug near the fireplace, while listening to the Isley

Brother's 3+3 c d, which led them to what they called the best love making ever.

"How do I let you go after that?" Rudy asked, nearly out of breath.

"That's a good question." Diara replied. And they slept before the fire.

Earlier that morning, Diara had opened the curtains to invite in the sunshine through a huge window that gave view of the entire living area from the outdoors, and a beautiful view it was. She had never enjoyed her home so much.

She surprised Rudy with breakfast. He was deeply moved by the spread Diara had prepared. There were omelets, waffles, scrambled eggs with cheese, bacon, three different types of sausage, grits and yes, homemade biscuits.

Is there anything this woman couldn't do? He thought. If this was a dream, he didn't want to wake up. He ate until he was satisfied.

After breakfast, they walked the grounds and talked, while stopping to kiss once in awhile. The grounds keeper saw the two of them embracing and changed his mind about asking them about LaQuincy's latest request, which was to cut back the begonias for the winter in order for them to grow beautiful and full in the spring. He quietly did his job and thought he would go to the house later. When they returned to the house, Rudy and Diara sadly discussed their departure as

Rudy made plans to go the nearest market. Rudy pleaded with Diara to pack her things and run away with him. He would risk it all for her, and he would love and take care of her for the rest of his life, he promised.

While Rudy was away from the house at the store, Diara contemplated the idea of running away with him. Breaking her concentration, the phone rang. It was LaQuincy calling to give Diara the details of his arrival the next day. His flight was due in at 10 a.m. He would catch a cab. LaQuincy was excited about finally getting home. Diara could hear the excitement in his voice, but he noticed the lack of excitement, and a hint of nervousness in hers, especially when the doorbell rang. She rushed him off the phone to answer the door, afraid that Rudy had forgotten something, and LaQuincy would know that he'd stayed. When Diara opened the door, she was relieved to find that it was the grounds keeper, Mr. Sumner. The phone rang again identifying a suspicious LaQuincy, who was wondering who might have been so important that she had to hang up to answer the door. Relieved as well to hear old Mr. Sumner's voice, LaQuincy told her to ask him to return later. He really wanted to talk. Lowering the phone, she explained to him that her husband was out of town and would be home the next day, and he could answer any questions he had at that time.

Mr. Sumner said, "I beg your pardon m'am. My son worked here today and thought he saw the two of you out for a walk earlier. Maybe he was mistaken. I'll just get him to finish up this evening and I'll return tomorrow. So sorry to bother you, ma'm."

"Oh it's okay. I'll tell him you came by," muffling the phone tightly, hoping LaQuincy couldn't hear him.

Diara mustered up as much excitement as she could on the phone with her husband, yet there was a burning sense of guilt she felt for LaQuincy, and heartache for losing Rudy, who she had fallen deeply in love with in only a matter of days. How could she let him go when he was the one who made her laugh like a teenage girl? He was the one who held her while she cried and revealed her every dark secret while lying comfortably in his arms. What would she do on the next day of her life? Could she go back into LaQuincy's world and forget about it all? Could she leave all of this for the sake of love, a love so perfect, yet so unforgiving? Those questions drifted through her head while saying goodbye to LaQuincy until tomorrow, and hello to Rudy until the end of tonight.

Chapter 5

Weeks had flown by since Rudy left and LaQuincy returned home. Rudy had gone back to Panama a few days after Christmas. They talked a few times and decided not to risk being found out by phone, since Diara had decided to stay with LaQuincy. Spring had welcomed its' beautiful colors of pine green on lawns and every other color imaginable in flower gardens. LaQuincy and Diara had gone back to living their lives as usual. Diara decided that the pains of leaving LaQuincy were much greater than staying, especially since no one knew that she and Rudy had shared a temporary love affair. In her heart, she would cherish him forever, feeling that if only for a short time, she had experienced real happiness. While she longed for his touch, she also secretly hoped that the love that grew inside her was from the greatest love of her life, and somehow, someday would connect them, yet LaQuincy doted and protected his wife. He treated her as if she was the most delicate flower ever grown, most of the time.

At the turn of fall, the Carpenters welcomed a healthy, beautiful baby girl in the world. Diara and LaQuincy were proud parents who couldn't get enough of this new baby. They played and cooed every day. Between night feedings and a demanding LaQuincy, Diara's hands were full. He had lain off the housekeeper, Joanne. He suddenly didn't feel the need to have one since Diara would be home indefinitely. More than ever, Diara needed help, but he didn't agree, even though they had always had someone managing the duties of the house. Since they had been married, Diara had worked very little. She did one photo shoot a month for Victoria Secret and Boston catalogs. LaQuincy had never even considered getting rid of Joanne. He wouldn't dream of Diara cleaning then, but now, she took it all in stride and didn't complain. She did it and did it well. Her home was just as clean as if a housekeeper had been there, with help. Diara remembered how angry Aunt Loody would get if the house was not cleaned to her satisfaction. That had been her first experience as a cleaning lady. The consequences were ten times more demeaning than the actual duty.

LaQuincy made reservations to go back to Boston for Thanksgiving again this year. He could hardly wait for his parents to see baby Christina. He didn't tell Diara until a week before they would be leaving.

He claimed that he'd forgotten and he added, "What difference does it make anyway? You have nothing else to do."

This was happening more and more, the sarcasm and belittling. One evening he told her that he would be glad when she lost weight.

"How long does it take for that fat to melt anyway? I didn't marry you for your looks, but I'll be damned if I'm going to watch you blow up right before my eyes. Trust me, it ain't a pretty sight."

Diara left the room crying that evening, but had to pull it together before their guest came. LaQuincy had a party catered for twenty people to see the baby, who was only three weeks old at the time. Diara was afraid to say that she wasn't up for company and that the baby was too young to be around strange people. She cringed and dealt with it while they touched her baby's cheek and breathed on her, but she was most determined that no one, not even LaQuincy would take Christina from her arms. When one of the ladies asked to hold her, Diara said that the baby needed to be changed. She quickly excused herself with her baby in arm and did not return until the baby was asleep. She received an angry look from LaQuincy as she walked down the stairs. After his guest left the house, he told her that she had embarrassed him and that she should have kept the baby downstairs since they were there to see the baby. Before she could explain that the baby was tired, LaQuincy turned her face toward his with a firm grip and said, "Don't let it happen again."

What had happened to change him so drastically? He'd become rude and moody and had frightened Diara a couple of times with a temper she didn't even know he had. It began while she was still pregnant. He never apologized for any incident. He just went from Jekyll to Hyde in seconds it seemed, and his anger was all aimed at her. This was not the man she married.

However, Diara looked forward to going to Boston for the holidays. They needed a change of pace. Maybe seeing the family would put LaQuincy back in his old frame of mind. She wanted her baby to feel the love of family, something she had not felt for years now. Mainly, she knew Rudy would be there. She heard LaQuincy talking to him on the phone. LaQuincy mentioned that Rudy had a surprise for the family. What on earth could that be, she wondered. They would all get there the same day, but Rudy would arrive a few hours later. Diara couldn't help but wonder if they would be able to hide their feelings on sight. One of his sisters had already had doubt about Rudy escorting her home. Diara didn't want to be exposed.

Chapter 6

LaQuincy's mother and father thought Christina was the cream of the crop. Dee held her nearly 3-month-old grandbaby and gazed at her in amazement. Once when LaQuincy was out of the room, Dee said, "This beautiful baby girl looks like her Uncle Rudy."

"You think so?" said Diara smiling.

"What's got you beaming like that?" LaQuincy asked as he reentered the room. "Mama must've said something great about your favorite person," he said.

"Uhm," said Diara, clearing her throat, unsure about what he meant.

Of course, Christina was her favorite person, but could it be that he knew that Rudy was a close second.

But before she could complete her answer, Dee said, "Yes, I was just saying how beautiful this baby is. She looks just like you guys when y'all were babies." Suddenly Diara became puzzled.

Why hadn't Dee repeated what she'd said? she thought. She didn't allow the thought to penetrate, but even if she had, she was now distracted by LaQuincy's sister Jackie, yelling, "Mama, I got your oldest son from the airport."

Dee quickly got up holding the baby and walked to the door. There stood Rudy in the door with his uniform on, more handsome than ever. LaQuincy and Sam were the first to greet him. Jackie took the baby and began to talk baby talk. Jackie and Krissy each had a son, Travis, 5 and Shane, 3 years old. Christina was the first child from one of the boys and the only granddaughter.

Rudy picked up his mother, spinning her around. Dee laughed as if he was the best thing she had seen all day. When the smoke cleared, so to speak, while hugging Rudy, Diara heard a woman's voice.

"Honey, which way to our room?" Before she could process it, Dee spoke softly,

"Hello there again Aaliyah," reaching to hug her. "Hello Mrs. Carpenter! It's so good to finally see your face," she said in a heavy Spanish accent, reaching to hug Dee back.

Who was she and how did Ms. Dee know her? Diara thought to herself while her heart sank. Her spirit was suddenly broken. She didn't know what to do with herself at that moment. She was thankful that LaQuincy had walked out of the room, or he would have known that she had been crushed by what she was sure was Rudy's surprise, which turned out to be his fiancé, the ex that he had told her about. Now they planned to be married sometime in the following summer. Why, she wondered, did he suddenly feel the need to get married now?

She was relieved though when she heard Dee say, "Aaliyah honey, your room is right down the hall here to the left," pointing in that direction. "Rudy, you'll be in your old room baby," she continued, while pointing in the opposite direction.

"Only married people sleep together in here," Rudy said mocking Dee to Aaliyah, who looked a bit dismayed.

"You got that right, son," Dee said. "Some things never change." They all laughed.

During dinner, Rudy tapped his glass with his fork to make an announcement after being nudged by Aaliyah several times. His eyes focused on Diara and vice versa while he broke the news about his engagement to Aaliyah. Everyone hugged again and welcomed Aaliyah to the family. Diara eased out of the room, using baby changing as an excuse. In the bedroom, she fought back her tears by holding her head down, allowing them to fall to the floor and not ruin her eye make-up that she had applied to perfection especially for Rudy. She stayed in the bedroom and rocked Christina until they both fell fast asleep.

Chapter 7

The next morning, Diara's feet were the first to hit the floor. Christina was ready for her morning feeding. Diara decided to make coffee for everyone while she fixed the baby's bottle. While she moved around the kitchen in an ivory colored, nearly sheer robe, she felt like she was being watched. As she turned to see who it was, the culprit spoke. It was Rudy.

"I still have never seen a more beautiful sight in all my life," he said.

Angrily, Diara snatched Christina's bottle and tried to walk pass him as he blocked the entrance to the kitchen. He wore a white wife beater under shirt, muscles bulging in his chest and arms.

"Dear God, this man is hard to resist," Diara thought as she tried to physically force him out of her way.

"Your fiancé is all you need to worry about," she said.

"What am I suppose to do baby, be alone? If I can't have who I want, I have to have who wants me."

"You know I can't…" Diara said before she was interrupted.

"Good morning you two," said Dee, entering the kitchen from another room. "Where's my beautiful granddaughter?" She continued with a smile.

"Oh she's up, in the bedroom with her dad waiting for this bottle," Diara answered, smiling nervously, hoping Dee didn't sense the tension in the room, or hear what was said.

"Yeah, I was hoping to spend some time with my niece today. You think that's possible D, uh Diara?" Rudy asked, hoping his mother didn't notice that he'd adopted a nickname for his brother's wife.

"Let me get her fed and dressed and I'll bring her right out," Diara said, passing him to go feed her baby. She could hear Christina crying before she got to the door.

When she opened the door, LaQuincy said, "What the hell took you so long? You know she's hungry," he said rocking Christina gently.

"I made coffee and talked to your mom for a minute," she explained.

As he passed the baby to her, he placed his finger on her head and shoved her, saying "Get a brain! You don't leave me with a screaming baby. What the hell do you take this for?" He grabbed a shirt off the chair, threw it over his head, and left the room.

Diara cried uncontrollably, feeding Christina and listening to her husband laugh and talk cheerfully with his family, as if nothing had just happened. Was she being punished for the sin she had committed? Maybe she had this coming. Could the decision to stay with LaQuincy be worse than the consequences of running away with Rudy? She was beginning to feel as though LaQuincy hated her, but why? Had he found out about her and his brother and decided to torture her? What was it? What had she done?

After calming down, Diara showered and dressed, and then dressed Christina and joined the family for breakfast. Rudy was the first to reach for Christina. He kept saying,

"She is just the prettiest thing." She smiled when he played with her.

"If I didn't know better, I'd say you've done this before," said Aaliyah. "Well not really, but it's not hard to love on a little precious lady like her," he said, raising her slightly above his head. "I think I'm in love," he said bouncing Christina.

"You'd better be," said Aaliyah, slapping Rudy's backside.

Everyone laughed, except Diara, of course. The day after Thanksgiving, Jackie and her husband David walked in. They had come to invite the young adults to a jazz club where David played the saxophone with a band called The MAXX. Diara had never met David. He'd played out of town during Thanksgiving the previous year. David and Jackie had met at a nightclub right after Jackie had ended a 4-year relationship with her son's father, Mallory. Travis was only two when Jackie married David. He loved David every bit as much as he loved his own father. David and his family took Travis in as their own. In fact, he was spending a few hours with David's parents while Jackie and David made their rounds that day. Krissy agreed to take Travis and Shane to a movie later. She wouldn't be attending the concert this time. She had heard David play numerous times before. Everyone else agreed to meet Jackie at the club to hear David's band. Dee and Sam were excited to keep their granddaughter. Dee held her every chance she got. Until it was time to get dressed for the outing, everyone relaxed lazily around the house, conversing and snacking. Dee's kitchen was filled with all kinds of good food. She was always sure to have her sons' favorite things to eat and drink.

Aaliyah was a talker. She held up any ear that would listen. Diara thought she was nice, but her stomach literally cramped when she thought about Aaliyah in bed with Rudy. She was a very attractive woman in her early thirties. She wore too much make up and it did little to enhance her beauty. However, her accent could be described as pillow talk. Rudy met her in the air force. She was a dispatcher for the Air Force Emergency Dispatch Center. He was attracted to her voice instantly after talking to her about a patient that had been admitted. He needed information about the time the phone call was received. He became so curious about the voice, he went to the Dispatch Center to put a face with the voice, and was pleasantly surprised to find Aaliyah. So, he introduced himself. He told her about the strong attraction that led him to her and she told him that her voice was one of the ones heard on Latin channels, commercials, introductions, promos. She did a lot of work on the side, speaking, but nothing big had ever come of it. Rudy was even more intrigued when he actually heard an ad that featured Aaliyah's voice. They dated on and off for three years, probably more off than on because Rudy couldn't commit. He really liked Aaliyah and her voice seemed to soothe his soul, but he was unsure if that was the voice he wanted to hear for the rest of his life.

Diara found herself in deep thought of Aaliyah whispering in Rudy's ear with that voice and imagined what would happen next. Even though she was afraid that LaQuincy or Aaliyah would notice that Rudy became captivated whenever she entered a room.

Hours earlier, he had quietly walked up next to her in the kitchen and said, "Not that you weren't perfect already, but you're even more perfect now, thanks to Miss Christina."

"You're kidding right?" Diara asked, sipping on a bottle of water.

"Your brother thinks I need to lose weight."

"He's a jerk," Rudy said as he walked away, heading to the next room.

LaQuincy and Sam passed Rudy coming out of the room. Sam stopped to talk to Rudy.

"Hey Diara, Let's go get dressed," LaQuincy told her.

"I'll be right there," she said. "I need to get the baby's things to your mom."

"I've given her everything. Now, let's go," he said.

"Let me just check on her, okay?" said Diara, a little perturbed about LaQuincy being so demanding.

LaQuincy didn't say anything. He just walked out, but Diara noticed that by the look on his face, he wasn't pleased. Shewent into the living room where Christina slept in a bassinette that Krissy had brought to Dee's house for her. Krissy and Dee sat and talked while Diara kissed her baby's cheek. She heard Dee tell Krissy that Diara and LaQuincy were such good parents. Once Diara was satisfied that her baby had everything she needed and told Dee a few things that might occur when the baby woke up, she went to get dressed for the club.

She was happy to find LaQuincy in the shower. She figured she might need to make up for what he might call blatant defiance a while earlier. It had been more than a month since they had slept together, and only a few times since the baby had been born. He hadn't even tried, which didn't bother Diara so much. Sex with him wasn't the worse thing, but incomparable to sex with Rudy, but she had made the best of it because she had to, as the man's wife. She undressed and walked into the shower.

"What do you want?" He asked.

"Isn't it obvious?" She asked, unveiling herself, throwing the towel over the shower door, smiling.

"Excuse me, I was just getting out," he said, looking at her in disgust, passing by her and closing the shower door behind him.

"Oh my God! LaQuincy, are you serious? What is wrong with you? Oh forget it!" Diara yelled.

Before Diara could get out of the shower, LaQuincy had dressed and was back to the living room stealing kisses from Christina. Diara dressed for the jazz club and went to kiss the baby good-bye as well.

LaQuincy insisted that the two of themride with Rudy and Aaliyah. She never stopped talking the entire trip to the club. When Rudy stole peeks at Diara, he could see the look of frustration on her face. He figured it was because of Aaliyah's non-stop talking. He hadn't a clue about the way his brother had just treated her. When they made it to the club, Jackie greeted them and led them to their reserved seats. David came over before the first set to speak to the family and welcome them to the show. Diara ended up sitting between LaQuincy and Rudy. The place was intimate and dark. Candles on the tables seemed to be the only light in the room, except on stage.

A server took their drink order and the band began to play. They sounded great, Diara thought. LaQuincy and Rudy commented about how impressed they were with David and his band. After a couple of drinks, Aaliyah stayed on the dance floor with or without Rudy, even with one of the band members. Surprisingly, the band played Brown Eyed Girl.

LaQuincy excused himself to go the men's room. Diara sat still, next to Rudy, wondering if he remembered the song from the cozy little steakhouse in the airport. Did he remember how Ronald Isley serenaded them through the night at her house, and the way they obeyed every lyric and created some moves of their own? Suddenly, she felt his hand slide into hers under the table.

"You remember!" She said.

"Of course I do! How can I forget?" he said, rubbing her hand softly and constantly, bringing back memories.

"I want you and my baby, Diara, to be with me." She looked at him in shock because he'd said "our baby."

"I can tell you're miserable D," he said. "Hell, I'm miserable, too."

"I can't do this Rudy." Diara got up and walked out. As she passed by LaQuincy, she said, "I need some air. The smoke is killing me."

"Okay," he said, and continued walking back inside toward the table.

She sat on a bench outside about 50 yards up a hill from the entrance of the club. After about 10 minutes, she heard Rudy say,

"So, you would let me marry a woman that talks that much? I saw how frustrated she made you in the car."

Looking up at him, laughing, Diara replied, "I have nothing to do with that. You chose her, I didn't. But seriously, she didn't bother me, even though she does talk her butt off."

"Yes, she does," agreed Rudy. "So what gives D? Why the sadness? You see, I know what it is."

"What, Mr. Know it all?" Diara asked smiling.

"Remember when you told me that if you study long, you study wrong and you regret the choices you make?" Rudy asked. "Well, you made the wrong choice in men, but it's not too late," he said smiling.

"As much as I love my brother, I would risk him never forgiving me if I could have you."

"We'd better get back inside," Diara suggested, suddenly standing, taking steps to pass Rudy and go back to the building.

"Is she mine?" Rudy asked. Silence covered the air and stopped Diara in her tracks.

"Let's go Rudy." Louder, he spoke again.

"Is she mine?"

Pausing for a few seconds, "Yes," Diara said quietly. He turned her around and pulled her close to him. They began to kiss roughly and carelessly as if they had nothing to lose.

"Well, I'll be damned," they heard a voice say.

Chapter 8

The family managed to make it through Thanksgiving, in spite of the club situation Diara and Rudy had encountered the night before. However, there was tension in the room. Diara was a bit on edge because of the news she had revealed to Rudy, and afraid of being exposed. Rudy kept wondering when the ball would drop as well, even though he couldn't pass by Christina without reaching for her. Just knowing she was his daughter was enough for him to risk it all, but this was neither the time nor the place. As satisfied as Dee was to have her sons at home, she knew there was discord in the family. She couldn't exactly put her finger on it, but she was very concerned about her sons. Aaliyah approached the family sheepishly, afraid to make eye contact with anyone. Last night was a blur.

Sam happily ate breakfast with his family and made light conversation. He was proud of the men that sat before him, his handsome sons who had made wonderful lives for themselves with beautiful women. He couldn't help but wonder how much he had contributed to their success, or if he had at all.

In the kitchen on Sunday morning, LaQuincy found his mother having coffee alone. As soon as she saw him, with her usual gentle smile, she asked, "What's the matter baby?"

"Nothing Ma," he answered. "I'm just dealing with some things right now. I don't know quite know how to handle them. I don't know what to do."

Throwing her arm around his shoulder, she asked, "Well sweetie, what can Mama do to help? Is it Diara, the baby, what?"

"Yes, no, Ma, I don't want to talk about it. I'm trying to work it out. Don't you worry about me okay, I'll be just fine. You just take care of yourself. Everything will work itself out, hopefully for the best."

"Son, why don't you talk to someone," Dee said, "Or better than that, you know I always say, take it to God in prayer, 'cause you know, nothing's too hard for Him."

"Yea, I know Ma and I will," he promised as he kissed her cheek and left the kitchen quickly to avoid any more questions. LaQuincy would definitely take Dee's advice on one thing; he would talk to someone about his problem when he returned home.

Later that afternoon, Dee and Sam said goodbye to their sons and family. Dee stood teary eyed, as she had always dreaded goodbyes. Sam stood stone faced as he tried not to allow his actual feelings to show. Show no emotion, feel no emotion, and you won't get hurt. He had taught his sons to be tough. That's what his father had taught him. Even though this was embedded in him, he had much regret about the things he taught or didn't teach his children. Sam had been a daily drinker, an easily angered drinker. His children had feared him with an unhealthy fear. He harbored regret about his present relationships with his children. He felt that they just tolerated him now. Sam was never sober enough when they were children to know their true characteristics, which left their talents and gifts uncultivated in their youth. He wished he had a second chance to make it up to them and to Dee, because now as an elder in the church, he was forced to face the ugly truth; that it was him who had placed the burden of a family curse upon them, leaving his wife to play a role as head of household intended by God for the man. Dee ran the home with love and protection as much as possible. She even disciplined when necessary, and all in hopes of not setting Sam off. His wrath caused years of heartache, and Dee was always doing damage control to keep the children in their proper places. "The Bible says to honor thy mother and father," she would tell them, and that alone instilled love and respect in them that even Sam didn't know they had.

Today, she resented Sam for those very reasons. She called it resentment to keep from going to hell. She thought about how his lack of parental leadership pushed her into a two-role position, and she couldn't fully give to her children the mother they deserved because she had to do Sam's job as a father, while he entertained his mutually drunken friends daily in a shed that he had built in the back yard initially intended for work.

She knew when she married Sam that he had some drinking issues and she figured they stemmed from his father's alcoholism, but he was a handsome dreamer. She had to believe that he was too ambitious to become consumed by anything that would cause him to become unproductive. She'd met him while on summer vacation. According to Dee, he was handsome and extremely smart. He had plans for the two of them. "He would give her the world," he'd said. He promised her parents that he would love, provide for and protect her always. However, her father gave her to him unwillingly and in full disbelief of Sam's empty promises.

Since her children had become adults, each problem or hardship they faced made Dee wonder if she could have made their road easier, had she been allowed to just be their mother. All arrows pointed toward Sam for the neediness, the selfishness, abuse and shame he had brought upon her family. So today, this small-framed, 66 year-old, fare skinned woman walked into her quiet and empty house silently, more willing to speak to the walls than to utter one word to Sam, who spent even more time in the shed to give his wife the one thing she wanted that he could always provide, his absence.

When Rudy and Aaliyah boarded the plane, Aaliyah wondered why he was so quiet, yet she dared not ask. She figured it was because she had embarrassed him at the club, even though she couldn't remember what happened, no matter how hard she tried. This was the first time she had met his family and she had once again let alcohol overtake her, but what had she done? She woke up in the same clothes she had worn the night before and was lying across the bed. She had a nasty hangover, which she thought led to her severe headache until she felt a knot on her head through her hair. There was even dried blood. Rudy was on the floor. It was obvious that she'd passed out and he had brought her to the bedroom. She had to do something. She couldn't go on this way.

She had noticed a change in her skin lately too. Even this morning, she could see the toll alcohol was taking on her. She was beginning to look aged and she wasn't old enough to experience such an obvious skin change. It was the vodka. She was sure of it. Rudy had no idea how much she drank, and she wasn't sure if she wanted him to know. They had made this grand announcement of getting married out of nowhere. He had just mentioned it to her on the flight to his parents' home. He thought they should just get married, like there was nothing else to do. There was nothing romantic about the proposal. In fact, there was no real proposal. She really loved Rudy, but she didn't feel that he ever really loved her like she'd always dreamed of being loved. Should she even begin to think of going into a marriage where there were already major problems? They had issues that had never been resolved. She had caught Rudy with other women on many occasions and snapped. She'd cut tires, poured paint on his car, and had even fought other women over him. Had he apologized for the way he'd treated her, coming back to her when other relationships didn't work out? No, yet foolishly, she would take him back. He knew what to do to get her back. He knew her body better than she knew it. No one had ever done to her the things that Rudy could do. On the other hand, she had lost herself and began to drink when he was on to something new. It was because of this relationship that vodka had become Aaliyah's confidante.

Anyways, she thought, I don't know if I want to marry him. As a matter of fact, I know that I don't. And when I get home, I have to tell him and find an AA meeting. I'm tired of making bad decisions and not remembering what I did the night before. I'm going to make a change that's best for me. "Thank you, God," she said to herself, lying back in her seat, feeling a sense of peace that only God above could give, for the first time in years.

Rudy thought about the night before. He knew now that he had a baby, a beautiful baby girl, with the only woman he ever really loved. He thought about their kiss before it was interrupted. He thought about the decisions that had to be made and knew the situation would get worse before it got better. He looked at Aaliyah, who slept so peacefully and thought with regret about the hurt that she would feel, once again, when he dropped this bomb on her. He had planned to marry her and do right by her, but Diara having his baby, changed the dynamics of it all. He hoped she would understand, but the odds were against him with her and most certainly with his brother. As hard as it would be for everyone, Rudy knew that he had to move fast before this all blew up in his face, and because he wanted Diara and Christina with him as soon as possible.

When their aircraft was about to land, Diara reached for LaQuincy's hand. He allowed her to hold one hand while he held the baby with the other. Afterwards, they moved quickly through the airport to make the next flight. Before they reached their seats, LaQuincy said, "I'm sorry about the way I've been acting. I really do love you and the baby and I'm going to see someone when we get home."

"See someone about what?" Diara asked. "Just things I'm dealing with. I know I've been moody and hard to live with and I haven't been my "sweet" self lately," he said with a smile, raising his fingers in air quotes.

"You're right," Diara said.

"Well I know it's my fault and I'm going to get myself together so that I can make you happy again. I want us to be a real family, a happy family, just the three of us. I love you!"

Diara listened, but she couldn't respond. She didn't want it to come back to bite her. She wanted Rudy to rescue her. She felt that LaQuincy was a time bomb. He had apologized before. It was beginning to be meaningless. She had no idea what he was going through and she didn't care. She lay back in her seat and thought about the flight that she and Rudy had taken together. That was who she wanted holding her hand on flights, and off.

Chapter 9

"Please come in Mr. Carpenter," Dr. Hampton said, shaking LaQuincy's hand. "I'm Dr. Melanie Hampton. Please make yourself comfortable there on the sofa," the woman suggested, pointing toward the mahogany leather sofa, while reaching for the miniature tape recorder on her desk. She was very attractive and so professional, LaQuincy thought, not exactly what he expected.

"I hope you don't mind if I use this device," she said. "I like to record sessions with my clients so that I can go back later to assess it. It will help me to serve you better. Please begin by explaining the best way you can, what brings you here."

"Well," LaQuincy began with a sigh, "It's a long story," he said, chuckling nervously.

"Well, Mr. Carpenter, we do have some time. Therefore, you can begin wherever you would like. If we need to extend your time, we will, or we can schedule as many sessions as needed all at once, or on a one at a time basis," explained Dr. Hampton.

"Okay, I would like to begin with the past year or so, and please Doc, call me LaQuincy," he added. Dr. Hampton nodded in agreement.

"I was married about a year and a half ago. My wife and I just had a baby. We're supposed to be happy, being newlyweds and all, but I make her miserable, and that makes me angry. Therefore I make her more miserable," said LaQuincy.

"Why do you think it's you that makes your wife miserable?" Dr. Hampton asked. "Well, it's because I have these ghosts from my past that continue to haunt me. They only arise when I start to enjoy my life. Next thing I know, I begin to make bad decisions and hurt the people around me, people that I'm supposed to love. I'm here today Doc, because I want this to stop. I want to fix it and make it go away, but I don't know how. And believe me I've tried."

Dr. Hampton listened carefully as the room became silent, then after inhaling a deep breath, she said,

"How long has this problem been rearing its ugly head?"

"Since I was about 13 years old," answered LaQuincy.

"What have you done to make it go away?"

"Nothing good, in fact, I'm ashamed to say," stated LaQuincy.

"Oh, well Mr. Ca…, sorry," she corrected herself, smiling. "I mean LaQuincy; you never have to be ashamed in here. Please feel free to say whatever you're feeling. I'm sure you'll find it to be liberating, even healing."

LaQuincy continued to talk to Dr. Hampton, but the session ended before the problem was actually verbalized, which was the intention of Dr. Hampton. She wanted to be sure that LaQuincy was completely comfortable with her before he disclosed too much information. She had had experiences with clients who changed their mind about therapy out of fear that they had told too much to a stranger. They wouldn't schedule more sessions, nor would they respond to the office calls her assistant made. However, this session had gone well. Dr. Hampton planned to revisit it by listening to it on her auditory device later after office hours. She would assess her scaffolding skills, or guided questions. Were they leading the client in the direction of disclosing relevant and appropriate information? She looked forward to more sessions with LaQuincy.

LaQuincy was pleased with his visit as well. He was comfortable with Dr. Hampton. He thought she was easy to talk to, and she was right, thought LaQuincy, talking was liberating, even though he had hardly hit the surface where his problems were concerned. However, he planned for more sessions. He was sure that with Dr. Hampton, he would get a breakthrough, as he heard his God-fearing mother mention on more than one occasion. He would learn to love Diara and the baby in the way that he thought they deserved.

Chapter 10

Rudy and Aaliyah had parted ways just as she said they would. Aaliyah wanted to be sure about her decision, so, she invited Rudy over a few days after Christmas to end it, especially after never receiving an engagement ring, and no more discussion of marriage. Rudy was surprised and because his male ego was bruised, he was even a bit upset.

What brought this on? Was there someone else? How could *she* not want him anymore? He begged to make love to her once more because he knew he could change her mind about the decision she wanted to make, but Aaliyah stood strong.

Her body screamed for him to grab her and just have his way but her determination to improve her lifestyle made her put her body in check. For the first time, Aaliyah was in charge. When Rudy left her house that day, she made a phone call to accept a job offer in New York as the new voice for Lexus commercials. She had auditioned on a whim months ago at the suggestion of a friend. She was shocked and excited to be able to say that she would be the voice behind one of the most popular luxury car brands in the world. Major corporations like Lexus usually hired accomplished talent, even Hollywood actors for voice over work. She was offered a three-year contract and was promised a great future with the company if all went well. A new start in life was just the ticket for Aaliyah and she could hardly wait to begin it.

Rudy had left Aaliyah's apartment feeling somewhat rejected, yet relieved at the same time. He had gone to her place to break it off with her and it had backfired. After giving it some thought, he was glad about the fallout. He had not hurt Aaliyah, and he found himself happy for her. She texted him and told him her good news and her plans to relocate. He was a little embarrassed about the stunt he'd tried to pull on her when he tried to coerce Aaliyah to give in to him. He laughed in an effort to convince himself that his actions were typical; part of the "guy code." He really wasn't sure why he acted that way toward the break-up with Aaliyah. He loved Diara. His whole focus had been about the two of them raising their baby together. He talked to her several times daily whenever LaQuincy was away at work. They made plans to be together for Valentine's Day, which wasn't too far off. Diara was scheduled for a photo shoot in Ocho Rios, Jamaica from February 12th to the 16th. Now that she was meeting Rudy, they had extended the trip for a few days, and Christina would join them. LaQuincy would be shooting for K Fashion Magazine in Manhattan that week. By that time, Rudy figured he would have a plan in place about how he and Diara would spend the rest of their lives together.

LaQuincy was going to visit Dr. Hampton for the third session this week. He felt that he was slowly getting to the bottom of things. He looked forward to solving the problems that had haunted him for so long. In the meantime, he knew he needed to follow Dr. Hampton's advice about watching his temper with Diara. It seemed that she knew just the right buttons to push to make him fly off the handle. She was always on the phone with her agent, looking for work, although it seemed that she would hang up abruptly when he got home. Part of him believed she was making plans to leave him, but he wouldn't jump the gun. That had made matters worse in the past. He noticed that she had become very distant and sometimes even cold toward him. Had he driven his wife to hatred? They had not had sex since before Thanksgiving, and even then, it was not worth writing home about. Nevertheless, it would be okay. He would make it up to her soon and they would love each other the way they did when they were first married.

Chapter 11

After seeing LaQuincy leave for work, Diara walked to the huge window in the living room, holding Christina in her arms. She gazed out at the wintry mix and hoped it would remain mild. In one week, she would be with the man she loved, and she wanted no interruptions. Before that thought could marinate in her mind, she noticed Mr. Sumner, the groundskeeper coming up the walkway with a large envelope in his hand. Then the doorbell rang. He claimed he had some important information for LaQuincy.

"Please have him call me as soon as possible ma'm," he implored, giving her a card with his number on it.

"What was that about?" She thought. He acted kind of weird toward her, but she decided to ignore it. She had too much to be happy about than to get distracted about the lawn. When he left, her thoughts immediately moved back to the time she would spend with Rudy in Jamaica.

The phone rang, breaking her concentration. It was Rudy. She carefully placed the baby in a playpen and answered the phone, smiling from ear to ear. "Hello my love," she said to him, while reaching for the rattler in the playpen, playing with the baby.

"Yes, I was just thinking about that," she said, "but I have to be optimistic. By next week, the weather will be wonderful. Our daughter will be with her dad and I'll be in his arms. After a short pause, Diara says softly, "I have to go my love, your brother is back."

"There she goes again," LaQuincy said to himself, "hanging up that phone again, but I can't worry about that," he thought. "I have a session with Dr. Hampton this morning and I can't be late."

As Diara walked toward him with her phone in her hand, he said, walking to the playpen, talking baby talk to Christina, "I forgot some of my camera equipment. I am shooting the governor this afternoon for the Signs Magazine."

"Oh yeah," she said nonchalantly.

"I'll see ya' later," LaQuincy said gesturing to kiss his wife's cheek. She turned her head. As hurt as he was by her blatant rejection, he walked out the door.

Dr. Hampton finished up with her last client and prepared her miniature-recording device for the next. As the client walked pass Dr. Hampton, she said,

"You look gorgeous today, Doc. Is your husband taking you out tonight?"

Laughing, Dr. Hampton replied, "No, Mrs. Pittman. I'm divorced. I have no special plans.

" Doc is always sharp Mrs. Pittman, said Delia; the doctor's assistant. She is the fashionista of this building," Delia continued. The two ladies smiled and looked on as Dr. Hampton blushed because of the compliment. As she walked away, Delia disclosed information about Dr. Hampton to the client, saying, "And child her husband left her because she can't have kids. It is not all about looks and prestige. Now, don't get me wrong, she's a good woman and she always drives the latest Jaguar, but when the rubber hits the road, a man likes to have a little look alike running around his house, and if a woman can't deliver, everything else is out the door."

"Well I happen to find that preposterous. I have been married to my husband for 32 years and we don't have a child in this world, because I was barren, but it never stopped him from loving me and he still does. I wonder what Dr. Hampton would do if she knew her own assistant was hating on her?," said Mrs. Pittman, "Be careful Ms. Delia, I happen to think Dr. Hampton is a fine woman, and God's got somebody for her that will love her in spite of her imperfections. Now you have a good day."

Today she wore a tweed skirt with a long sleeve, button down collar shirt, slightly hidden by a black blazer that complimented her full figured hips and small waist. The five-inch black pumps added length and definition to her already muscular legs. This five foot six chocolate bombshell demanded attention. Gently pushing her swooped bang behind her ear to meet the bun in back of her head, she stepped outside her office to collect a chart on her next client and there he stood; LaQuincy. Looking over her glasses, Dr. Hampton took the chart from Delia's hands and couldn't help but notice how professionally dressed LaQuincy was this morning. It was strange for her to notice because she had a rule that she followed religiously, *the no face rule.* Each client was seen as a problem that she would tackle, one at a time. The no face rule kept her from looking at her male clients as potential mates. These people had too much drama. She wanted to fix it, not become apart of it.

When Dr. Hampton and LaQuincy walked into the office, Delia said to Ms. Berry, a client of another counselor.

"He sure is fine! I wonder if he's single."

"Child," said Ms. Berry, "I've been married so many times, I don't even look at men like that anymore, but he caught my eye. Yes ma'm, he is easy on the eyes."

Dr. Hampton gave a welcoming smile to LaQuincy as she closed the door behind them.

"Get comfortable there, Mr. Carpenter. Sorry, I mean LaQuincy" she said, noticing his expression about the last name thing, while skimming the chart in her hands.

"The last time we met, you were discussing some details from your childhood that led to an incident. Let's go back to the shed where your father entertained his friends. Is that a good place for you?" She asked, looking over her glasses again.

"Yes, I believe I was telling you that it was frequent. My mother hated it and so did we, my siblings and I," LaQuincy explained.

"Why did you hate it?" She asked. "Well for one, my old man would get angry after drinking so much and he would come in looking for a reason to beat my mother," he said pausing.

Dr. Hampton allowed the silence and LaQuincy spoke again at will. "I don't like remembering those times because the kid I was couldn't protect my mom, and she was so sweet and kind; still is." Again, silence flooded the room.

"What do you think you would have done if you could've protected her?" Dr. Hampton asked.

"I would've; I don't know what I would've done. My dad is not the same man anymore. He stopped drinking about seven or eight years ago and I watched him change. He has taken on my mother's spirit and I can't help but love the man. I can't hold a grudge when the man is different, can I Doc?

Everything's different now, but there's an open wound that hasn't healed in me, and probably the same for my siblings as well, or at least one of them for sure." LaQuincy said sadly.

"Tell me how you got this wound, LaQuincy," the doctor said, in a persuasive tone. "Feel free to relax. You can lye back if you would like, close your eyes. Just get comfortable," she suggested. He rested his head on the back of the sofa and closed his eyes.

He began the story of a night his dad had friends over, out back, in the shed.

"It was a cold Friday night in January. Every day might feel like Friday to a person who doesn't go to a job, but Fridays were celebrated by these men like they had accomplished something great during the week. Not one of them worked. They just showed up and drank; during the week too, but on Fridays, they were louder, more rowdy and they stayed later, much later." LaQuincy recalls on this particular evening that his father, Sam had come inside the house and told Krissy, who was eleven at the time, to bring cups, ice, sodas and water out for him and his visitors.

My mother was a nurse and worked the night shift several times a month. This night, of course was one of those times," he said regretfully. "When Krissy came back inside, she told me that she was very uncomfortable about the way one of the men had looked at her. She said she had never seen him before. I had just completed a speech for the freshman debate. I was running for president of student council. To ease her mind, I asked her to listen to my speech. She gave me a few pointers. Imagine that; a 13-year-old getting ideas from an 11 year old, but that was because she was so smart. Krissy was known for being a creative genius, even at her age. We called her the female Doogie Howser. Our older brother and sister weren't home either. Rudy played basketball, and they were in the state tournament. We knew he'd be late getting in. Jackie baby-sat on Fridays, so we had no idea what time she would be home. Therefore, we ate and went in the family room to watch television.

"It was normal for my father's company to come inside to use the restroom once in awhile. They didn't talk to us and we preferred it that way. I assume the week had worn us out, and we both must've fallen asleep, one on the couch and the other on the loveseat. I woke up to muffled screams and my sister was gone from the living room. I ran in a panic, following the sound to the tragedy that I knew was behind it. In her room that I burst into, a man was raping my little sister on the floor. She was face down, screaming for her life, looking back for me to save her. Immediately, I began to pull him, but he wouldn't stop. He appeared to be a giant over Krissy, muscles everywhere. He pushed me off as if I was as light as a feather. I kept coming back, hitting him with all my might. He didn't budge. Suddenly, I was hit so hard in my face that I was knocked unconscious. When I came to, my pants were down to my knees and blood was coming from my sore rectum. And Krissy…" He paused, realizing his phone was vibrating.

"What about her, LaQuincy? What about Krissy?" Dr. Hampton said, urging him to continue. "Yes," he said, answering his phone wiping tears from his face and clearing his throat, looking up as if he wasawakening from a bad dream.

"Uhm, I'll be right there." As he hung up the phone, he said, "I have to go. That was the producer for Signs Magazine.

They're interviewing the governor this afternoon and I'm doing the shoot."

"That's wonderful LaQuincy," she said.

"I shouldn't have come here," he said. "And you're wrong about something Doc, I don't feel better, I feel worse and I never want to talk about that again. I never want to talk to you again. You have a good day," he said as he snatched his coat from the sofa, rushing toward the door.

"LaQuincy, please don't go. Believe it or not, you are making progress," she said in a hurry to beat the slamming door. "Wow," she said in amazement, "that poor man."

Chapter 12

At last, the time had come. Diara was becoming so anxious about seeing Rudy; she pretended to be sick the entire previous week so that LaQuincy would know that sex was out of the question. She kept her hair wrapped and tied in a scarf and wore flannel pajamas to bed to insure no easy access. He had even helped her to bed one night from the sofa because she told him she was too weak to get there alone. She had advised him to sleep in the guest room so that he wouldn't catch what she had, but he wouldn't hear of it. He stayed in the room and took care of Christina while Diara rested quietly each night until the day came for them to part ways.

He noticed the burst of energy she suddenly had the morning of her departure. Rudy had texted her earlier as she stepped out of the shower, telling her that he was in the room, that it was beautiful and Joanne's room was adjoining. This was just the most exciting day that she'd had in a long time. It would still be hours before she could actually see him, but she wanted to look her best even in traveling gear. She wore a new black Nike jogging suit with Kelly green stitching. The tight fitting t-shirt was Kelly green with a black waistband meeting the green band on the yoga pants. Her hair was straight, but bounced with her every move, full of body.

When LaQuincy insisted on taking them to the airport, he wasn't surprised when his wife refused his offer. She wanted to leave her car at the airport because she was due back sooner than he was, she said. LaQuincy would be leaving for Manhattan a day later than Diara and the baby.

"So when will you return from Rios?" LaQuincy asked while placing her last bag by the door.

"I'll be back on Friday if all goes well," she answered.

"What about you? She asked.

"Oh I'm not real sure. This is a package deal. I'll be shooting for several departments in the K building this week," he explained.

"Oh, well, I guess this is good bye for now," she said, reaching out to hug him.

"Wow, this feels like I'm hugging an old friend. That's all you got, girl? The old pat on the back hug," he said. "Have we really come to that?" he asked.

"Well I don't know LaQuincy, have we?" Turning away from him, Diara says, "I'm going to get the baby from her bed."

"Hey, what is that you're wearing?" He asked. Diara looked surprised. Agitated, she stopped, turned around to face him and asked,

"What?"

"You smell good. Come here, let me smell it again," he said. Reluctantly, she walked toward him. He met her near the staircase and opened her jacket. To her surprise, instead of smelling her neck, he began kissing it.

Calmly, at first, Diara said, "No, LaQuincy, I have to go. Joanne is traveling with us to watch the baby while I work and I have to pick her up."

"You'll have time," he said, whispering in her ear. "You put me off all week, and I see you're back to your old self this morning now that it's time to leave. Damn girl, you're even glowing. What the hell is that about?" he said, getting louder. "Do you know how long it's been since I've slept with my wife?" That's when she noticed how tightly he was holding her.

Starting to resist out of fear now, Diara yelled, "Let me go, LaQuincy. I don't have time for this. Please, I told you I'm in a hurry," she begged as she began to cry. LaQuincy ignored her and ripped her t-shirt open; exposing a black satin bra lined in red lace. "Oooh nice, that must be new," he said. The more she resisted, the angrier he became. They tussled, knocking over a sculptured piece that LaQuincy had brought from Italy before meeting Diara.

"You bitch!" He yelled, punching her as if she'd broken the statue purposely and singlehandedly.

"Please LaQuincy," she begged, "don't do this."

The look in his eyes let her know that this would not end soon and it would not end well. Her struggle was getting harder. She was losing ground and he was now tugging on her pants. He pushed her down so hard that her head bounced on the marble floor and hit again. Then he pulled her pants off.

That's when he saw that she was wearing the matching black satin thong and garter; also lined in red lace. Kneeling over her on one knee, he said, "Someone was about to have a good time with my wife," unfastening his pants with one hand and holding her down with the other he said, "but me first," He continued and she just lay there, screaming and crying profusely, "NO! I hate you!"

Chapter 13

"Mr. Carpenter right?" Alex, the receptionist greeted LaQuincy as he entered the building. "Welcome to Manhattan and to the K Company, right this way, please, sir. Here is your agenda. You have a meeting with the crew in the Madison Room at nine. Enjoy your stay," she said, turning to leave him, after showing him the meeting room..

As the day progressed, LaQuincy became more and more amazed by his assignments. He was in the big time now for sure, rubbing elbows with high dollar celebrities and using state of the art equipment. He stayed at the New York Palace, an Iconic, and Manhattan Luxury Hotel located just steps from the Rockefeller Center on Madison Avenue. He was busy. People praised his work and he was happy at the moment. He could almost forget the mess he had left at home. Almost.

Each day had its own excitement and reasons to be thankful. LaQuincy had received a surprise phone call from Rudy and tried to tell him all about his busy, yet exciting schedule, but Rudy seemed anxious and said he was only calling because he had called the house and didn't get an answer. He hadn't heard from Rudy in a while; but was touched by his brother's concern for his family, although he had to lie about his wife's well- being.

On Thursday at one, LaQuincy left a Fashion Showcase that featured wedding gowns and diamonds for the occasion.

Then he was off to shoot a layout of Lexus. K Company Business Magazine was doing an interview with the president about one of the most recognized luxury cars in the automobile industry. The final question was, "Who voices the new Lexus ads?" The president informed them that she was in the building. A pretty young lady walked onto the stage. Instantly, the interviewee was intrigued by the distinct voice behind the car company and asked the young lady to give a sample voice over of the way she promoted Lexus automobiles. As soon as LaQuincy heard the voice, he quickly moved the camera from before his eyes and sure enough, it was her, Aaliyah, his brother's fiancé. What a coincidence, he thought. "How did she get here," he thought.

The interview lasted about a half hour, and he almost missed the chance to speak to Aaliyah, but after he packed up the equipment for his next photo shoot, he ran outside to find her. Just before she ducked into the limousine, LaQuincy called her name, "Aaliyah!

"Oh my gosh, what are you doing here?" She asked, walking away from the limo, to hug him.

"Well, I just shot your interview for one thing," he answered.

"Seriously, was that you?" She asked, giggling.

"Yes, small world, huh?

You look a little different." He replied.

"I hope that's a good thing," she said, smiling.

"Of course," he said, "you look great."

"Thank you," she said, "So how long are you herc for? I'd like to show you around the Big Apple if you feel like hanging out, or did your wife, Diara right, and baby girl come with you?"

"No," said LaQuincy. "They didn't come with me. So, you live here now?" He asked."My brother didn't mention that," "Well yes! It's a long story," said Aaliyah, "but I'll tell you all about it later, over dinner maybe. So are we on for tonight?" She asked.

"Sure, that'll be cool," said LaQuincy.

"So where are you staying?" Aaliyah asked. I'm at the New York Palace, Suite 1102," he answered.

"Wow, the Palace, huh?" She said. "Ms. Kennedy knows how to treat her people, doesn't she?" Aaliyah joked.

"Yeah, I guess you could say that," said LaQuincy, smiling bashfully.

"Okay, I'll pick you up later," she said, waving as she got into the limousine.

In the meantime, Rudy had finally gotten some relief after speaking to his brother. He had desperately tried to reach Diara for days, but after finding out from LaQuincy that she was home in bed with the flu and the housekeeper, Joanne was there to see after her and Christina, he realized she was in no condition to talk and certainly not to travel. Yet he was puzzled because she had been so excited. She had said nothing about feeling ill. Here he was on this beautiful island all alone.

"I have to see her," he said. "My brother won't be back for days. I'm catching the next flight out." He packed his bags and headed for the airport.

However, the only truth LaQuincy had told was that Diara was home in bed, but not with the flu. She was depressed, and suffering with migraine headaches from a mild concussion, and a fractured jawbone. Joanne was caring for her and Christina. She had taken Diara to the emergency room the night of the incident, trying hard to convince her to tell the truth about what happened to her and press charges against LaQuincy, but she just sat there, unresponsive, tears falling from her eyes, one at a time. She had shut down the way she used to do when Aunt Loody had one of her moments of rage and abused her. She wouldn't talk to anyone. She refused to allow anyone to help her. The staff at the emergency room begged her to cooperate with them. It was their duty, one of the nurses explained, to report abusive situations, "Please ma'am, don't let him get away with this," she begged, but Diara wouldn't budge. After a couple of days, Joanne had finally gotten her to put something on her stomach, and even then, she only took a few sips of broth from some homemade chicken noodle soup, but to Joanne that was at least a start.

Chapter 14

Aaliyah and LaQuincy had decided to eat before perusing the streets of the city in Aaliyah's 2012 Lexus IS C, luxury convertible. She suggested Robert DeNiro's restaurant, Tribeca Grill. . The place was popular and notably good. During dinner, they discussed the Thanksgiving visit in Boston and laughed about Aaliyah's black out the night they went to the club. LaQuincy explained that he only laughed because he could relate. "I've been there, done that," he said. Aaliyah wanted to know exactly what happened that night. She figured since he had been the only one who was completely sober, that he was the one to ask. LaQuincy told her that he saw her walk outside with two of the members from David's band. As strange as he thought it was, he didn't question it. However, a half hour later, Jackie was sending for him to come quickly because she was unconscious, and they needed to go.

"Did we go to the hospital?" She asked.

"No because you started coming around. My brother told us that you had done it before and we didn't need to worry, so we went home."

For the rest of the night, Aaliyah was in deep concentration about parts of that night that were still a blur. Why couldn't she remember? She and LaQuincy ended the night after sightseeing and talked about getting together again before his departure.

LaQuincy had enjoyed the night with Aaliyah. She had confided in him about her bumpy relationship with his brother and her newfound sobriety. He was happy for her, however, he didn't think he wanted to see her again. He had bigger fish to fry. He had called home several times and Diara still wouldn't talk to him. Should he just face the fact that it was over between them? Or was there still a chance for their family? Wouldn't she want to try for Christina? Surely, she wouldn't take his baby, his only reason for not breaking under pressure. But then again, there is another man involved. She was on her way to him, with my baby in tow. I just know it, thought LaQuincy. "Still, there is no excuse for my behavior. No matter what, I had no right to treat my wife that way. I can't blame her if she wants to leave me, but I hope she'll stay."

So tonight as he lay tossing and turning, he found himself following his mother's advice. He kneeled down beside his bed and began to pray. "Lord, I have heard all my life that nothing's too hard for God. This mess I'm in will put that phrase to the test." He continued to pray throughout the night, later realizing that sleep tonight was probably not an option.

After leaving LaQuincy, Aaliyah thought about that night in Boston. She realized that through drunken bad judgment, she had walked outside with the two band members to smoke marijuana. She felt so ashamed, she cried herself to sleep.

"Oh God!" Aaliyah said waking up in the middle of the night. "It was not a dream. I did see the two of them kissing and the baby is Rudy's. Oh no!" she cried as she lay in her king size bed wondering how to handle this disastrous situation. Suddenly she became restless and crawled from under her purple satin comforter, pulled on some skinny leg jeans that lay on her red velvet bench at the foot of her bed, reached in a drawer and grabbed a t-shirt that exhibited a Lexus logo. With tears streaming down herface, she continued to moan while reaching into her closet to retrieve her flat suede black ninja like shoes.

"How could you do something like this Rudy?" She said aloud, while pulling her shoes up onto her feet. "I knew you loved women, but this is too much even for you. Is nobody off limits? Damn you!" She screamed. "I finally remember. Now it's so clear." She said out loud while turning on the bathroom faucet for the towel she'd gotten from the linen closet. Then she brushed her teeth, gargled mouthwash between cries to keep from getting choked and wiped her face once again. She looked at the clock. It was three o'clock in the morning, she thought, "but this is the city that never sleeps, and I need a drink." She walked back to her bedroom, put on a baseball cap, snatched her keys from the kitchen counter top and rushed out the door.

Chapter 15

When Joanne answered the door at Diara and LaQuincy's house, Rudy was there. He told Joanne that he heard she was caring for his sick sister- in- law. "I wanted to check on the flu patient," he said with a smile.

"Flu patient?" Joanne said. What flu patient?" "I'm LaQuincy's brother and he told me that Diara was home in bed with the flu," explained Rudy.

"Well your brother is either lying or he doesn't know," Joanne said.

"Know what?" Rudy asked, becoming anxiously concerned. "Come, see for yourself," Joanne said, turning her back to lead the way to Diara's bedroom up the stairs.

Joanne opened the double doors to the master bedroom and allowed Rudy to enter before her. Diara was asleep. He could hardly believe his eyes.

"Who did this? Was there a break in? What? " Rudy asked.

"She won't say, won't talk to anyone," Joanne said.

"And I don't mean any harm. I know he's your brother and forgive me if I'm wrong, but I believe he did it. That's just my theory."

"No," said Rudy. "I don't believe he could do something like that, but let me talk to her," he said, walking Joanne to the bedroom door.

Diara slowly opened her eyes as he approached the side of the bed. As soon their eyes met, she began to sob. Rudy's eyes suddenly filled with tears as well as he sat on the bed to comfort her, her head buried in his chest, they cried together.

"Talk to me baby," he said softly. "Tell me what happened."

She described verbatim, the traumatic attack she had endured at the hands of his deranged brother. Rudy expressed to Diara deep feelings of hatred for LaQuincy and how he wanted to kill him for what he had done to her. Nevertheless, Diara finally convinced him that it wouldn't be wise and would only make matters worse, for she knew there was still trouble ahead.

He carried her down the spiral staircase in his muscular arms like scenes from the movie, An Officer and a Gentleman, and told Joanne that he was taking Diara and the baby away for a while until things settled down. Joanne kissed the baby and hugged Diara, bidding them farewell.

After Joanne left, they packed a few things for her and the baby. Diara knew she would never see this house again, and she was satisfied. She had been rescued by her knight in shining armor.

Even in the condition in which she was found, for the first time in her life, she felt safe, and she was happy, even in a state of turmoil. The white house had been tarnished. Saying goodbye to it and its contents was long overdue.

"Please forgive me Lord," she said, "for I know that I have sinned, but I have to tell you thank you for not forgetting about me and my baby and for the blessings that you have bestowed upon us at such a time as this, even if for only a while, in Jesus' name. Amen."

LaQuincy had fallen to sleep at peace. He would fight to make things right with Diara. He would go back to his sessions with Dr. Hampton and learn about the inner rage that consumed him. He wanted a better life and to be more in control of his emotions than vice versa.

He was suddenly awakened by loud knocks at the door. "Was there a fire in the hotel?" He thought, while rising swiftly out of a deep sleep. "Why else would someone beat the door down like that?" He wiped his eyes and opened the door.

"What the...," said LaQuincy. "So you knew?" Aaliyah yelled tearfully.

"Knew what? What are you talking about?" LaQuincy asked.

"Come in, come inside please," he said, concerned, but still barely awake, pulling her in his room by her arm. "You'll wake up everyone on this floor. What are you yelling about?

"Rudy and your wife, that's what," she blurted, going into the bathroom for a tissue to blow her nose.

"Girl, what are you talking about? Rudy and my wife? What about them?" he said.

"I finally remembered," she cried. You remember when I kept asking you to tell me about that night?" Before he could answer, she said, "Well, I finally remembered. I walked outside with the two band members to smoke and when I finished. I saw a man who looked like Rudy up the hill near a tree. He was missing from the table when I came off the dance floor. I was sure he was in the men's room, but, anyways," she said, blowing her nose again, "Their backs were turned to me, and they didn't hear me. When I saw her, I started to join them because I knew she was family. Being drunk, I thought nothing of it. Then I heard her say they needed to go back inside, and just before I said something to them, he said, "Is she mine?" I hid behind the tree. I was curious then, okay. Sue me. The second time he asked, she said "Yes," and the sudden silence made me walk around the tree. They were kissing, LaQuincy," she said.

"What do you mean is she mine? That doesn't make sense," he asked. "Your daughter, I guess, what else?" Aaliyah answered.

"None of that's true. Did my brother hurt you that bad, that you'd tell a lie like that? And I see that you fell off the wagon," he said, while reaching for his phone. I'm going to give Rudy a call and let him know he has a bitter woman on his hands, who can't seem to get over him." When Rudy's phone went to voice mail, he left a message for his brother to call him ASAP; he had some info that he would surely want to hear. Without Aaliyah being aware, he called Diara's phone as well, which also went to voicemail. He claimed to be calling Rudy's phone again. He grabbed Aaliyah's arm, squeezing it hard and said, "Get out and don't come back. Maybe you play these weird games with Rudy, but you will not include my family."

Aaliyah gave him a strange look and said, "I'll go, but something in you believes me. I don't know what it is, but you know I'm not lying about this," she said.

He slammed the door behind her, yelling, "Get out!"

First, he covered his face with both hands, took a deep breath, as his body weakened, and fell against the door. Then he got up and paced the floor, taking long strides across the room. A glass vase filled with roses that sat on a round wooden table was slammed against a wall, shattering to pieces, coinciding with a shout from LaQuincy, "NO…!"

Chapter 16

Rudy and Diara flew quietly across the country, her head resting on his chest, both only reacting to the babbling of the busy little six month old that he held in his lap. Rudy's silence was out of anger for LaQuincy and for himself. This did not go as planned.. His plan was incomplete, but he was working on it. Even thoughit worked itself out, she got hurt. Now he would protect her and Christina from here on in. LaQuincy will never hurt her again, or I will kill him, he thought.

Aaliyah had tried to call Rudy's phone several times, but to no avail. It continued to go to his voicemail. As much as she hated him right now, she wanted to warn him that LaQuincy knew about the affair. She sensed rage in LaQuincy's eyes. Something told her that he had already suspected his wife's infidelity, just not with his own brother.

She was sorry she had gotten involved, but as usual, when she drank vodka, she did things that she lived to regret. She was shocked, but she shouldn't have reacted so carelessly, she thought, because she and Rudy had already ended things. Diara was just another person he had cheated with; only this time, he had a baby.

"Umph, umph, umph," she groaned, suddenly angered by her thoughts. "He made such a fool of me, and so did she, pretending to be so innocent when we were in Boston. They all doted on her, probably because I was the loud mouth and she was so meek, the tramp. I'll bet the two them laughed at me for not knowing, for not remembering. Ooh, I feel so stupid. Well, I guess they'll get what's coming to them, won't they? I'm staying out of it."

LaQuincy missed his first appointment, which was at 7am. Alex, the receptionist had been instructed to locate him. The CEO at the K Company had finally been notified that LaQuincy Carpenter, the top camera operator had not shown up for work, had not called and had left his hotel room, with damages that would be added to the K Company bill. Little did they know, he had caught a red eye home to Chicago. While they questioned his whereabouts, he was pulling his bags off the belts in baggage claim at the O'Hara Airport in Chi Town.

When he walked into his home, the quiet and chill of the house spoke volumes about the information he had learned before daylight. He dropped his bags and ran up the staircase, pushing open the double doors that revealed an empty room and an unmade bed. He went to the closet, but couldn't tell if anything was missing. Maybe, she had taken the baby out for a while, and she'd be back shortly. They could sit down and talk and she could clear up this lie that Aaliyah had told about her having an affair with his brother, and most especially about his baby not really being his. He walked into the nursery and many of the baby's things were missing, but that didn't mean they were gone. He wouldn't lose it this time, he promised himself. Before the next thought, the doorbell rang. "Maybe that's them. She forgot her key," he said running downstairs in a hurry to open the door. But it wasn't Diara and Christina; it was Bill Sumner, the grounds keeper. He was holding a huge envelope.

"Mr. Carpenter, I'm sorry to bother you. I came by a while back and asked your wife to tell you I stopped by. I owe you a huge apology, actually. My son worked in my place one day, months ago, before the Christmas holidays. He moved out a while back and I found this DVD in his bedroom with your name on it. I wanted to know what he would have that belonged to you. So I put it in the player and I'm sorry to say that it's a tape of you and your wife. I can't apologize enough. It looks like he was outside your window. It has a date on it. I, I don't know what to say, Mr. Carpenter. My son's behavior is unacceptable," he whined. "I hope you won't hold this against me. I promise to never allow him to work for me here again." LaQuincy stood dumbfounded as he slowly collected the envelope. He assured Mr. Sumner that nothing had changed and he could continue to work as usual. He could hardly wait to close his door and put in the DVD.

Chapter 17

Diara found herself settling into Rudy's world quite easily. His place was nothing like she was accustomed to with LaQuincy but she was beginning to see a brighter future. He was attentive, witty and loving, just as he'd been before. Daily he nursed her back to health. She had daily therapy for the cracked jawbone and constant observation for the concussion. He really was the medicine man, she thought, as she remembered him referring to himself when she first met him. In fact, he would be graduating the following spring. He would finally be Dr. Carpenter. He planned to practice medicine for a few years under mandate of the Air Force and then he would be able to venture out wherever he chose to reside.

Rudy tried to be cheerful in Diara's and Christina's presence. However, he was full of resentment toward his brother. He saw that LaQuincy had tried to contact him a few times. There was no way LaQuincy could know about him and Diara unless Joanne told him, and after speaking to her, she hadn't seen or heard from LaQuincy so he then wondered what else his brother could want to discuss with him. LaQuincy had only left one message, but it didn't sound urgent, and Rudy wasn't ready to talk small talk with his brother.

"I'm sure he probably doesn't know where to look for Diara, but he should know that she had every right to leave. Maybe he'll just let her be," Rudy thought. Then he thought about Christina and realized that there was no way he would let her just take the baby and run. He needed to be prepared, he thought. There's no telling what LaQuincy might do.

Aaliyah couldn't wait to get off work this afternoon. She had a pounding headache. She had been yelled at a couple of times today for not following the script properly. She found it hard to concentrate. She wished she had not drank the night of her new revelation. It had put her in a spin, back at ground zero and she could do nothing to stop it. A bottle of Grey Goose Vodka sat on the table in her condo, half full, and it was all she could think of today. She was as excited as a kid on Christmas day when Omar, her supervisor told her to go home, get some rest and be ready to focus tomorrow. "This will be my last day drinking," she promised herself, as she had the day before.

Days on end, LaQuincy watched repeatedly, the DVD that Mr. Sumner had hand delivered to him. It wasn't him and his wife like Mr. Sumner assumed. It was his brother and his wife making love in his house. He had cried until he had no more tears. As he lay down the phone after booking a flight back to New York, he went to the hall closet and took a black leather box off the shelf. Inside the box, there lay a Browning Hi-Power 9 millimeter pistol on a red velvet bed of the box. While loading it, he took a trip down memory lane and reminisced about the moment his brother met his wife. He remembered Rudy turning his head when he was affectionate with Diara. His brother had agreed to fly home with her without hesitation after Thanksgiving last year. In fact, it was his idea. LaQuincy thought. That's when he made his move. Did he plan the whole thing? Was this about hatred for me, or was my wife so irresistible? he said, putting his fist through a wall.

During his layover in Atlanta after the America's Top Model shoot in California, LaQuincy had lunch with his friend Terrence, who mentioned that he had seen the two of them in the airport and thought Diara was Rudy's wife. And Aaliyah, poor Aaliyah, thought LaQuincy, found them together and couldn't even remember. She even heard them discuss the baby's paternity and saw them kissing. The betrayal goes deeper than that, he cried, as he remembered his brother's so-called concern of his family's whereabouts just earlier this week.

"Now, I realize he only called because she didn't make it. She was meeting him in Jamaica. I knew there was someone else. I knew she had been touched. She never responded to me the same again after I returned from LA, and that's why I hated her. But I was willing to forgive her and try to work my way back to loving her. I would have never, in my wildest dreams believed, my own brother. How could he do this? he thought. How could she? "DAMN YOU BOTH," he yelled. He picked up the phone once again and dialed 911. "I want to report a kidnapping," he said, and held the gun to his head, crying, believing it was best to end it all.

Chapter 18

After another trying day at work, Aaliyah was glad she had made it through the day and was even more glad to be home. She fixed a drink as soon as she got into her condo. She changed into some cut off blue jean shorts and a half shirt, threw on some ankle socks and put on a Jennifer Hudson CD. She chilled at the tall two top table by herself as if she was in a bar with a room full of people. She listened to the music and swayed back and forth with her eyes closed. After a couple of drinks, Aaliyah convinced herself that Rudy's parents needed to know what Rudy and Diara had done. She made the call and spoke to Dee. Before she began to tell her reasons for calling, she asked Dee to forgive her, for she meant no harm, she just felt that any mother would want to know about something this threatening to her family.

She told Dee about seeing LaQuincy in New York and that he was the one who helped her to remember the night at the club when she discovered the relationship between Diara and Rudy, and about the baby. Dee was devastated, of course and wanted to know where her sons were. Aaliyah didn't have an answer for that. Therefore, Dee hurried off the phone with her. She had some calls to make. Afterwards, Aaliyah fixed another drink and questioned whether she made the right decision in calling Rudy and LaQuincy's mother. She sounded weak, unlike the jovial little lady she had seen last

Thanksgiving, but she didn't dwell on it, she put on the latest Charlie Wilson CD, and just before she sat down again, her doorbell rang. She looked through the peephole, and saw LaQuincy.

Snatching the door open, she asked, "What are you doing here?

"Whoa, you look horrible.

What's going on?" "I needed to apologize to you," he explained. "You were right about my brother and my wife," he said.

"How did you come to that conclusion?" she asked, walking toward the stereo to turn the music off. "What did you do?"

"I see you've been drinking," she said.

"I didn't do anything. Here," he said, giving her the DVD of Rudy and Diara.

"What is this? Do I even want to know?" She asked, walking toward the television, inserting the DVD.

Gasping, Aaliyah said, "Is that," she said with hesitation at first, "yep, that's Rudy," she said finally recognizing his face.

"Oh my! Get that out of there. I don't want to see that. How could you watch another man with your wife? Don't answer that," she said, walking past him to turn the music up. "I'm going to finish my drink. You obviously can use one too." LaQuincy waited for the DVD player to open, then took out the DVD. After carefully placing it back in the envelope in which it was delivered to him, he joined Aaliyah at the table. "So where'd that tape come from?" She asked, while handing him a drink. For the rest of the evening, they talked. He cried. She comforted him. He had no plans to return to work right now. He had missed several days without contacting the K Company with any explanation, so he figured it was rather pointless to call them now. They had probably already replaced him, he figured. And by then, he was sure that reputationwise, he'd been blackballed.

Before the night was through, as usual, alcohol took control of Aaliyah. She danced until she was hot and sweaty. She spunaround once and ended up falling into LaQuincy's lap. She laughed and saw that he was smiling for the first time since he hadarrived. To LaQuincy's surprise, she kissed his lips gently. When he barely responded, she took his hand and guided it to touch her in places that really surprised him. She kissed his lips again and finally he kissed her back. Then, she stood and led the way to her bedroom and LaQuincy followed. He handled her roughly, almost angrily. He ripped her shirt off and picked her up; placing one of her breast in his mouth, sucking like he'd never had the pleasure before, from anyone. They kissed hard and Aaliyah wrestled his shirt off and then his belt. His baggy jeans seemed to fall to the floor as if they had been ordered to do so. She seemed to enjoy the roughness, as she returned it with bites to his neck and scratches on his back. She whispered to him, calling him Papi, telling him how much she wanted and needed him at that moment. Neither she nor he bothered to remove her shorts. His manhood found its way through a side entrance passing the shorts and her thong, making her scream for mercy as he entered. The more she moaned and squirmed, the deeper he entered, while walking toward the bed to lay her down. The kissing and hard thrusts from LaQuincy continued and Aaliyah took them, living happily in the moment. Veins visibly showed on LaQuincy's forehead as he reached the point of explosion joined by sheer delight according to Aaliyah's mouth to his ears.

LaQuincy wasted no time leaving. He picked up his pants, fastened them, grabbed his coat and walked out the door just as quickly as he had entered. Aaliyah was sound asleep before the door closed.

Dee was in a tizzy after talking to Aaliyah. Her blood pressure was already too high and she just didn't feel well today. She needed Sam's help this time. This was his one shot at helping his family through a crisis. Dee had always dealt with her children's problems, big and small. She would've loved to jump in and solve this problem as well because she knew the severity of it. She prayed for God to shed some light and fix this problem between her sons and she knew she had to trust that He would do it because she was dealing with her own crisis this time.

Jackie had just brought her home from the doctor's office before Aaliyah called. She had pretended that the visit went well but the truth was that she had been self-medicating a foot ulcer that eventually caused severe tissue and bone damage to her toe. Her toe would need to be removed as soon as next Tuesday. The doctor warned her that the surgery was needed quickly or her foot, and possibly part of her leg would be amputated in less than a month.

She sat alone in the dark in her living room and she called out to Jesus. She prayed aloud and her voice rang throughout her house like a bell calling in emergency. Sam listened from the kitchen as if he were listening to angels sing his name. He joined her. He fell to his knees before her and he prayed with her. He prayed for her and he begged her forgiveness. Although apprehensive at first, she finally accepted her husband's embrace.

They talked and cried, and years of paralysis from countless disappointments that had them bound, were released. They clung unto each other as if in a storm until they met the love they had known before. By daybreak, she believed again, the promise that Sam had made to her father many years ago. She trusted him. She loved him. Now, they could face together their inevitable tragedies, for God had granted them a peace that surpassed all understanding.

Aaliyah wasn't surprised when she woke up and found LaQuincy gone. She had an excruciating headache. The night before was a blur, as usual. The last thing she remembered was dancing in front of LaQuincy, trying to lift his spirits. She hoped she did, but she had no idea what time he had left, or how they parted. Looking down at a bare chest, she thought she had gotten too drunk to complete the task of taking off her clothes.

"I can't do this anymore. I need help," she said in a shivery voice, taking her cell phone off the charger and dialing.

"Pam," she said, "I'm in trouble. I haven't been to a meeting in a couple of weeks, and I fell off the wagon after some heartbreaking news. No excuse. I know better than to allow anything to affect my sobriety. But I need you or I'm going to fall even harder."

After pausing for a moment, Aaliyah thanked her partner from AA and called to her job to let them know that she would be in the next day. She found some clothes to put on so she would be dressed when Pam got there. She ran a hot shower and began to cry as she finished undressing and stepped inside.

Chapter 19

Diara had experienced another nightmare that caused Rudy to stay home from work again. She lay quietly in his arms, rocking Christina to sleep. When the phone rang, it was Dee, his mother. He could tell by her voice that she had heard the news about him and Diara. LaQuincy had spilled the beans, he thought. "I'm sorry Mother. I don't know what to say, but I can't talk about this right now. Diara was abused and she's not in the best condition. The baby is doing great. I have them both here with me and I'm going to protect them. I promise to get into this with you at another time real soon and I'll answer every question you might have."

"I love you girl; you know that," Rudy said to his mother. By the way, how are you?" "Not great," Dee said. "I have to have surgery," she said. "What?" he said, alarmed. Rudy walked into another room, away from Diara. "Do you need me Mama? You know I'll be there if you need me. I know you and Dad haven't been…" He stopped speaking and listened to his mother explain that she and his father were doing fine and all she wanted him to do was straighten out things between he and his brother, "somehow, someway," she begged. He promised he would.

When he returned, Diara could see that he had received troubling news.

"What's the matter, Sweetheart?" She asked. "Nothing for you to worry about," he said.

"How are you feeling today?"

"Thanks to you Dr., I'm feeling quite well today," she said, walking to lay Christina in her crib. "My head doesn't hurt this morning. I want to get out of bed and do something for you", she said, reaching for his hand. "I mean, you've been so good to me. You've been caring for the baby and me since we got here. You haven't even been to work. I don't want us to ruin things for you. I want to be good for you. Now tell me what's wrong," she said as he laid his head in her lap.

After a moment of silence, Rudy said, "Baby, some may say that this is all wrong because of the way we came together, but you and that baby have changed my life," he explained. "I never loved anyone like this before. And if that's wrong, I don't want to be right," he said, laughing about the song lyrics he used. Diara chuckled slightly as well.

"Seriously though, I want to give you the world, and if you let me, I promise I will," He said.

He rose up to kiss her. Then slowly they began undressing each other, gazing into each other's eyes as ifthey were afraid to look away, and for the first time since they had reunited, they made love.

Chapter 20

LaQuincy had not worked in months. Daily, he received notices about unpaid bills. His mortgage was now five months behind and he had ignored the foreclosure proceeding notices that had been piling up lately. His contracts with the K Company and Models Inc. were null and void. He had managed to be replaced on even the minimal photography gigs he'd had on the side, such as shooting award events on the red carpet. He made money taking unusual and natural shots of celebrities in their day-to-day lives that he sold to the most popular tabloids in the business that earned him hundreds of dollars a day. His skills were in high demand. Unfortunately, none of it meant anything to LaQuincy anymore.

He was back where he belonged, he thought, in his own private drunken hell, having a pity party. He would tell anyone who listened.

"Who in the hell did I think I was," laughing at himself, "thinking I could have it all. Take the car, I don't care," he said, staggering to the end of the porch, talking to the fellow in the tow truck who came to repossess Diara's car. "Hell man, take all of them. What do I need with a Ferrari? I bought that Cadillac for my wife. She ran off with my brother, took my baby and there's nothing I can do about it. It's been six months and I have not heard from them since. Oh, oh, yes I did. I got my divorce papers. That's right. They're in there on the table. I hadn't even looked at them. My baby will be a year old in another month or so, and I can't even tell her happy birthday," he said smiling. They disappeared and changed their phone numbers," he said, turning up a bottle of gin.

"Sir, I'm so sorry to hear that, but can you get the keys for me please," said the tow truck driver.

"Yea, hold on. I'll see if I can find them," LaQuincy said walking back inside the house. The man met him at the door to get the keys "I'm sorry you're down on your luck right now brother. But things will get better. I know all about hard times, but I know a man name Jesus who can make it all right again. He can and He will. Put that bottle down so you can think clearly again and give him a chance."

"Naaaaa, I been there, done that. It doesn't matter anymore. That's what got me here right now."

"Trusting God is what got you here?" The man asked. "I don't know if I can believe that one brother," he said.

"Okay, I'll say it like Adam said, "it was that woman He gave me," mocked LaQuincy, while holding his drink up, doubling over in laughter.

The tow truck driver shook LaQuincy's hand and walked back to his truck, saddened by the story that he could plainly see was only in the midst of its downward spiral.

Aaliyah was back at work on top of her game again. She attended AA meetings regularly and had received an award and a huge bonus from Lexus for her hard work. Today, she was meeting a realtor after work who would show her a fairly new, spacious two bedroom, zero-lot home in Manhattan. She had taken the virtual tour and liked what she saw. She daydreamed about the questions she would ask the realtor. She wanted to be in a neighborhood well- serviced by public transportation so that she could commute by bus, train, and ferry, quickly, easily, and affordably.

She would inquire about the surrounding public schools that offered students a well-rounded education and myriad special programs in the arts, sciences, law and other special areas of interests. She wanted the residence close to hospitals and healthcare. These days, she had a different outlook on life. She was more serious than ever about her sobriety and had even become a supporter of new members.

"Hey gorgeous," a male co-worker, Bernie, said to her, snapping her back into reality.

"When is that baby due?"

With a smile, rubbing her stomach, Aaliyah said, "My son is due Dec 1st."

"Well, you look absolutely beautiful," complimented Bernie. "Thank you Bern!"

Dee was happy, for the most part. She'd had the surgery and was healing well. Jackie, Krissy and Sam waited on her, hand and foot. Sam had begun to use a hidden talent that Dee had no idea about. He could actually cook. He created meals from diabetic cookbooks and made them as tasty as possible for his wife to enjoy. Many times, they'd eat by candle light and talk for long periods at a time. Dee worried secretly about her sons. She and Sam would discuss the problem vaguely, but Sam's answer to everything these days was prayer. "It changes things. You know that," he'd say.

"That's why we are here together in love again, because of prayer. A situation like the one our sons are dealing with requires prayer. There's nothing else we can do. They are adults now. You can't protect and shield them anymore, dear. Grown people make their own decisions, and many times we know what they should do, but they won't listen anyway, so we have to ask God to shield and protect them, speak to their hearts and help them come to their senses," he'd say. "Everything has to be done in God's time, not ours. We have to trust that He will make it better. You, in the mean time, have to concentrate on getting completely well. That is my total focus, you," he'd say with a smile.

Dee hugged her husband and thanked him for caring for her, and then as she thought of her sons, she'd realize that Sam was right and she'd pray.

Months had passed and Diara and Rudy found themselves more in love than ever. Christina was walking and getting into everything. Rudy's ceremony was coming up and he wanted to surprise Diara. He had bought her a beautiful long, velvet hot pink gown with a deep dip in the back that complimented her curves. She was scheduled for a makeover the morning of the ceremony at the newest and most popular one stop boutique in Panama City called Taylored for You, named after the celebrity herself, Taylor Drew. Christina had a pink and white formal dress with ruffles and white ruffled socks with white patent leather shoes. She had big curly locks like Diara. She was as pretty as a picture and her parents were so proud. Diara was as proud to be with Rudy as he was to have her by his side. He thought she was flawless. Because they were such a handsome couple, they caught the eye of everyone at the ceremony. When Rudy's name was called to receive his award, he called Diara to join him at the podium. There, he surprised her by getting down on one knee, asking her to marry him before his fellow airmen, their mates or spouses, and other officers of the Air Force. After she answered yes, while blushing shyly, he slipped a 2-carat diamond ring on her finger, turned to the audience with a huge smile, shrugged his shoulders and said, "The lady says yes, so you're all invited. Invitations will be coming soon." Diara smiled big and waved at everyone while walking off the stage.

As soon as Diara's divorce was final, the two planned to make their wedding a priority. Rudy wanted to give Diara a dream wedding. He could finally afford to do so.

It was official; he was now Dr. Rudy Carpenter, an Air Force Officer and medical professional. Many opportunities came with such an accomplishment; the chance to live, work and travel worldwide, 30 days of paid vacation each year, tax-free food and housing allowances, top-notch childcare centers and a huge increase in pay with many other benefits and advantages in place as well.

In three months, he would move his family to New Mexico, where he'd be assigned for the next two years. He and Diara had decided to take advantage of the travel opportunities. However, his final plan was to move closer to his parents. As awkward as the situation may have begun, he thought, his parents had always loved Christina and he wanted his daughter to be near her grandmother someday.

Chapter 21

A couple of years later, in Mexico, Rudy and Diara prepared for their second wedding anniversary celebration. Rudy rented a beautiful ballroom on the local base that seated fifty people. Joanne had come to live with them to care for Christina. Although she was three years old, Rudy didn't trust that Christina could communicate well enough in Spanish to tell if she was mistreated. Joanne didn't hesitate when they asked for her help. She had always wanted to travel and had no strong obligations to keep her in Chicago. Her only son was married and lived in Denver. Their visits were far and in between. Therefore, she saw no reason that they couldn't visit wherever she was. The Carpenters were moving to Europe in a couple of weeks, and Joanne was excited to join them. She adored Diara and the baby, and had grown quite fond of Dr. Carpenter as well.

The morning of the celebration, Diara fingered through the wedding album, reminiscing. They had married a few weeks before they moved to New Mexico. The wedding was a dream for Diara just as Rudy had promised, and she was a stunning bride. The newlyweds were still in awe of one another and their hearts were filled with joy, even if Rudy's family had decided not to attend. He wanted to fly his parents in to Panama City for the big day, but Dee and Sam agreed that it wouldn't be fair to LaQuincy. They had no choice but to accept the couple's decision, but they didn't feel that they should play a part in it.

Besides, they had not been able to locate LaQuincy in over a year. He spoke to his mother at length about the situation with Rudy and Diara. He was devastated. Dee could tell by the slur in his words that LaQuincy was drinking heavily again, but she said nothing because she understood his pain. She wished she could take it away, she thought, as she silently cried, listening to her adult son wallow in his own tears. She begged him to come home, and he said he would soon, but his cell phone was disconnected shortly after that, and she hadn't heard from him since.

They had contacted Red Cross, but with no luck thus far. Not knowing where her son was, kept Dee a bit uneasy. Sam was just as worried but he tried to be strong for his wife. He felt he owed her that.

Jackie and David went to Chicago to retrieve many of LaQuincy's belongings. Sam and Dee had received a phone call from the repo man a few months after LaQuincy lost touch with the family. After he spoke with LaQuincy the day he repossessed Diara's car, he went back to check on the fellow a couple of months later, he told Dee, "but he was gone, so I tried the door and when it was unlocked, I went inside, looked around the house for him, and found an address book. Your phone number was labeled, Momma, so I called it. I tried to minister to your son, Ma'm, but he had lost all hope. I truly hope you'll find him. He was pretty loaded when I saw him," he said.

As thankful as Dee was that the man seemed to care, she was still skeptical, as any mother would be. David agreed that he and Jackie should fly to Chicago to find LaQuincy and rent a moving truck to get his possessions out and store them.

But, looking for LaQuincy in the big city of Chicago was like looking for a needle in a haystack. After staying in his house for nearly a week, in hopes that he'd come home, David and Jackie had to get back to Boston. David's band was leaving for a twenty- five city tour in less than a week and Jackie had to work.

Jackie was proud of her brother's accomplishments, as she looked over his house at the beautiful pieces of art, marble floors, the winding staircase and cathedral ceilings. She cried at the thought of his heartache becoming heavy enough to make him just give up. "Was all of this in vain?" she questioned, still looking around at his exquisite possessions. "Was he at a point of no return?" she asked, and then she prayed.

Movers came days before they left, and so did another foreclosure notice. They spent days, making phone calls to his job sites, friends, business and all other contacts in his address book, but no one had seen or heard from LaQuincy in months. It was like he had dropped off the face of the earth.

"Where could he be?" Jackie said to David, through falling tears.

"I don't know baby," and he rocked her in his arms.

"How could Rudy do this to him?" She asked.

"What kind of woman brings this kind of pain to a man's family? Why couldn't she just move on to someone other than his brother if he wasn't enough for her? Doesn't she know you reap what you sow?"

"Unfortunately, so does the other brother," said David.

"God help them," Jackie whispered and nestled in her husband's arms.

Chapter 22

Aaliyah played on the floor with two-year-old Lance. He squealed with laughter when she tickled his belly. Then she'd pick her son up and hold him above her head, bring him down slowly only to repeat the tickles and giggles. Finally, the game would come to an end and Lance would know it was his bath and bedtime.

He would have to attend day care the next day, although he hated parting from his mother. Aaliyah hated being away from her son just as much, but tomorrow she had a doctor's appointment. She needed to know why she was experiencing such harsh abdominal pains. She tried to ignore it, but now her gums were starting to bleed heavily and she was experiencing sudden nosebleeds. She had even noticed that she was having problems thinking clearly, which was beginning to affect her work.

She had no family in Manhattan so she relied on the childcare center in the neighborhood to care for her son. She only worked three to five hours a day, so he was never there very long, but he threw terrible temper tantrums every time he went. The ladies at the center always told Aaliyah that her son adored his mother, and she replied by saying, "Yes, he's the only man who lights up when I come into a room." She'd laugh and as he'd run into her arms, she'd spin him around, with his arms around her neck and a smile as bright as the sun.

"Excuse me," the lady said to the gentleman sitting on the bench outside the federal building.

"Oh my gosh, can this really be you? I've looked everywhere for you. I was so afraid that something like this would happen. You seemed so vulnerable, like you were headed in the wrong direction the last time I saw you. Please talk to me," the lady said, taking a seat on the bench.

The man was dirty and his unshaven face gave him a sort of untamed appearance.

"Who are you?" The man asked. "Oh yeah, you're that doctor I was seeing. How are you doing there doc? What are you doing around here? This is no place for a lady, you know. Is that your car over there?" He asked, pointing to a candy apple red 2013 Jaguar.

"Yes, that's my car. Would you like to take a ride with me?"

"No disrespect," he said, "but no I wouldn't. I would like to do just what I'm doing, minding my own business."

"Are you sure about that?" She said. "There are some people looking for you." .

"Looking for me?" He asked. "Well, you tell them all that I don't want to be found," he said angrily. "Now leave me alone. You and they are better off without me. Trust me. I'm damaged goods. I ain't going to get no better, but at least I know it and I ain't bothering anybody, so go on now. Get out of here. It's dangerous down here at night," he said getting up walking fast toward some steps going down toward the gutter, so she thought.

Dr. Hampton decided not to follow him. She immediately returned a phone call to his sister, Jackie, who had called her while she and David were in Chicago looking for her brother. She wanted to relieve his family of the negative thoughts families encounter when a loved one is missing. She promised Jackie that she would keep in touch until she had more information. And she did.

She found him every day after that, as if he were her special mission in life, but after two weeks of getting pushed away, she had nearly changed her mind about going to the lowest parts of downtown to help a hopeless man, but that would be the day, of course, that he would look for her. He waited around for her because he missed her, but she didn't show. He finally realized that she was only being kind. There was no other reason for her to come to such a place. "What could a woman like her want with a lowlife, homeless drunk like me?" He thought and hated himself all over again for treating her so harshly. Had he learned nothing? He couldn't blame her if she never came back.

He only had enough change in his pocket to get a 40-ounce beer that day. Just as he was about to rise from his unkempt area and head to the corner liquor store as he had done daily for nearly a year, he saw a beautiful pair of snakeskin shoes, then a matching snakeskin purse. By the time he was on his feet, he was greeted with a smile from Dr. Hampton.

"Hello LaQuincy," she said. He just stood there, speechless, unable to hide the happiness he felt in his heart because she was there. Finally, the words managed to come from his mouth.

"Hello Doc!" He said, smiling.

Chapter 23

"Hawaii, here we come," said Diara, talking to Joanne, as they jumped up and down holding hands like children. Rudy was asked to take a job as the Director of Medicine and Research at a Medical College at a Military University in Hawaii. His salary would double and the house, which they saw via satellite, was a mansion, with seven bedrooms, eight and a half bathrooms, and an 1100 square foot ballroom, a huge theater and game room. They lived the life that high ranked officers lived while in Europe, but things were getting better and better, thought Diara.

When Rudy came home, Diara had cooked his favorite meal to congratulate him on his promotion, but it was nothing new. She cooked special meals for him nearly every night, with pleasure. Other times, he was taking her to dinner and dancing at the classiest officers' clubs on the base or to an evening event at someone's house. He showered her with the best of everything; clothes, shoes and jewelry, and Christina, with everything a little girl could ever hope for. Every day, as soon as he walked through the door, he'd kiss Christina. Then Rudy and Diara would kiss like they were kissing for the very first time, no matter who was around. Many times, they would ask Joanne to take Christina out for a walk. Joanne would laugh knowing that a kiss like that could only lead them straight to the bedroom, and she was right.

They had made wonderful friends that had children Christina's age, some older and some younger. There were always huge dinner parties. The children and adults went somewhere several nights a week. The families were all close knit and would hate to see the Carpenter family leave, although they promised to visit.

Dee was relieved that LaQuincy was back in touch on regular basis again. She could tell that he was on the road to redemption. "He talks about God every time we speak, Krissy," said Dee. "It's his whole conversation,"

"That's wonderful Mom." She could tell that Dee was ecstatic. "You finally got through to him," Krissy replied.

"I guess so," said Dee, with a smile of satisfaction. "I hope Rudy will come back to God someday soon. And hopefully he asked God to forgive him."

"I'm sure he has Mother," said Krissy.

"I would think that every mother's dream would be to see her children saved by God, and able to function well in this messed up world we live in," continued Dee.

"I think you're right Mother. It's exactly what I want for my son, and for both of my brothers. I am so glad Quin is doing better. He's had some serious, ugly issues to deal with in his life, especially for a man, and I knew, that like myself, that he would never get it together until he faced his demons and got some help."

"Yea, you mean what happened between him and Rudy? Oh, I think he's gotten over that," said Dee.

"Well, that's not exactly what I meant, but let's just go with that. I have to go," she said grabbing her purse and coat in a hurry. "I have to pick up the boys from soccer practice at 7:00," Krissy said.

"What do you mean, girl? What kind of issues are you talking about when you say, especially for a man?" She asked, while grabbing Krissy's arm.

"Mom, let me go. I promise to talk to you later, but right now I have to pick up the kids." Dee was distracted by Sam entering the room and let Krissy go, while staring her down like a gunman on a western movie. Everyone knew not to bother Dee Carpenter's boys, even her daughters.

Sam had fixed a baked salmon dinner smothered with apple chutney served with broccoli and new potatoes. He reminded Dee that the BET Awards were on television tonight. He wanted to be sure she wouldn't mind eating in the living room on a TV tray so they could enjoy the show. LaQuincy had been the reason they got hooked on shows like BET awards, Grammys, Emmys, ESPYs, whatever. If it was an awards show, they watched it. He had been the key camera operator for the show or the main photographer on the red carpet for years. They would always get together with Jackie, Krissy and their sons and yell, "There he is." Sometimes they would wait for him to call with the celebrity list of all of the big wigs he'd captured on camera. But tonight Dee and Sam watched because they liked the show, and they liked reminiscing about their son once being a part of the action, and they spoke of it with the same pride as if he were still behind the scenes.

Chapter 24

"Stand up sir in the back. Would you like to introduce yourself?" A counselor from AA said to LaQuincy. "Yes I would. My name is LaQuincy Carpenter and I am an alcoholic. I've had many rock bottoms, as have many of you and for years, I didn't know why. I've hurt a lot of people and of course, I've hurt myself. If I'm going to be honest here, I have to say, I hated myself. For most of my life, I have abused alcohol. It was my way of leaving myself, without dying. I suffered a traumatic experience in my early teenage years. I was raped and because of that myth that society has placed on men, that a man is not to suppose to cry, I held it in and it ate me from the inside out. I covered an open wound with a band-aid, thinking it would get better, but the band-aid was gin, vodka, you name it, I drank it. It was available. My old man was a drinker. That's what put me in that position to begin with," he said.

"I was angry," LaQuincy continued. "I brawled regularly, and for the dumbest reasons. I wrecked cars. I even injured someone once while driving drunk, and what did I say? I think you all know." And the audience said in unison, "I'm never going to drink again." "See, I hid that thing so deep," he said, "that I told myself, it didn't happen. I wished it had not happened, but since I've been in therapy, I've learned that it wasn't my fault. I couldn't keep making that my excuse for being a failure. It wasn't my sister's fault. The person that did that to us was a sick individual who had access to children because the adult, no, not just the adult, but my father, who was supposed to protect us, was more into his drunken friends and their partying than he was us. It all happened so fast. I couldn't have stopped it," He said.

LaQuincy was crying and many people in the audience cried as well. And after a long pause, he raised his head and said, "He raped my sister, right in front of me. I tried to help her, and that's when it happened to me. I blamed her for years, just like I blamed the man and my father. I felt like she was the reason that happened to me. I didn't think about how she felt," he said, as he put his head down to cry. "Yea, well, anyway," he said wiping away his tears. "That's the demon that brings me here, again. This is only the second time I've admitted this to anyone," he said, looking at Dr. Hampton, who sat at the back of the room, with tears falling, reaching in her purse for tissues. She had come with him as support.

He was in therapy twice a week with Dr. Logan Ashton. Dr. Hampton had referred LaQuincy to a list of therapists in the city and he had made his choice, and seemed to think he was making progress. Dr. Hampton had built a six-figure practice with a huge waiting list. Since she and LaQuincy were getting to know each other on a personal note, she knew it would be a conflict of interest to continue seeing him on a professional level.

However, LaQuincy was opening up to her more each day. In fact, she was unloading her baggage on him as well. She told him about her failed marriage and the reason she would never have children. Her abusive ex-husband had kicked her in her back when she was five months pregnant. Her water broke and the placenta separated from her cervix. He left her to die, and she may have bled to death had she not crawled to a phone to call for an ambulance. She was told by a doctor at a local community hospital that she would never have children. That was the moment she knew she never had to question how LaQuincy felt because he showed her by taking her into his arms and telling her how sorry he was for what had happened to her. She was all he needed, he'd said.

"I do want children some day," she said. "Don't you want more children?" "Well...," before he could answer, Melanie said, "I know the story about your daughter, and I'm sorry about that, but there are children out there who really need a mom and dad. I think you'd make a great dad."

They laughed and talked over dinner several evenings a week. Her honesty was attractive to him. He felt that she was trustworthy. He could tell her things he had never found a reason to share before and talking about his idiosyncrasies freed him, the same ones that continued to lead him back to the bottle. He couldn't believe he talked so comfortably with her. They talked like they'd been friends for life. Most people meant nothing to him. He was finding out that he had never really loved Diara. She was a piece of art, a trophy. She made him look good, like he was a success. In his business, that was important.

After the meeting, they went to dinner. In the car on the way to the restaurant, Dr. Hampton asked, "Did you ever apologize to your sister?"

"Yes, I did, a few months ago. We talked in depth about it. I asked her if she knew I blamed her, she said yes, and that's why she kept the secret about me. We only told my mother what happened to her, and she didn't stop until she had Jarred Cunningham prosecuted," LaQuincy said. "Will you ever tell them, your family?" She asked.

"I'm not sure? What do you think, Dr. Melanie Hampton?"

"You're free right?" She said.

"I don't know. Am I?" "You can be," she said,

"Come with me. I have someone for you to meet."

Hawaii was just what Rudy knew it would be. He was living his dream, making more money than he ever imagined and busier than ever. He would send Dee and Sam at least a couple of grand a month. They wanted for nothing. His parents were proud of their son, the doctor.

Diara tried modeling again, even though from the looks of things, the end of that was fast approaching. At the last shoot, she heard the photographer call her "the older broad." That was devastating, and she had no shoulder to cry on.

She missed their friends in Europe. Even Joanne had stayed behind. She had been dating a Navy officer before they left, who proposed to her the night of the Carpenter's going away party. Joanne was just as surprised as Diara and Rudy. That made leaving nearly depressing, especially for Diara. Rudy hated to leave Joanne, but he was excited because he was about to embark on a career he'd been after all of his life. Ten-year-old Christina would miss Joanne terribly, but she looked forward to meeting new friends and going to her new school. Diara spent most days, home alone, eating and watching TV. She was gaining weight, getting bored and her mind was beginning to wander. Rudy couldn't go out the door without her accusing him of going to visit his girlfriend. No matter what he said, she didn't believe him. Rudy continued to work out, and seemed to look even more handsome with age. The ladies at the university thought he was something special and many of them tried the normal female trickery to get his attention, but he let them all know that he was a happily married man.

"You never spend time with me anymore," Diara whined. "What is it? Have you found somebody else?" She asked.

"No, baby," he tried to assure her, but to no avail. "Why would you think something like that?"

"Everything is different. You don't make love to me like you used to. You're always late coming home and you claim to be too tired to take me places anymore. I don't blame you. I'm fat and I don't have anything going on for myself. You're this big time doctor and professor, and I'm just a nobody," she cried, while throwing her glass against the wall.

"Baby, you're still everything to me. I don't want anyone else. I love you okay. I tell you this all of the time. I don't understand what's going on with you, D. Don't blow this baby, please. We have a good thing here. You never were this insecure and I got to tell you, it's getting old. You do need to find something to do because…, " He said.

"See," She yelled, cutting him off. You do think I'm a nobody. You think you're better than me. I know you work with all those other professional women and you wish you had married one of them," she shouted.

"No, that's not true. I never look at other women like that. You're all I need. I just think you should get out more. Honolulu is the most beautiful place. Get out and make some friends. Come on now; promise me, you'll give this a chance. We have another year here and we can go anywhere we want. We chose this life together, remember? Christina loves it here and I'm trying to give you the world girl," he said.

"I don't want the world. I just want you," she said. "You have me. I don't know what else to do," he said, and left the room.

"You can stop lying," she screamed. Rudy kept walking, while shaking his head.

Chapter 25

Aaliyah hung up the phone and fell to the floor, crying out as loud as her feeble voice could sound. She was out of breath from walking Lance to school. Her kindergartener knew only bits and pieces about his mother's illness, but it saddened him to see her so weak.

She'd had one unsuccessful liver transplant and the phone call she received was to confirm the failure of the second. Before picking up Lance from school, a friend took Aaliyah to her doctor's appointment where she was given the most dreaded news ever. According to herdoctors, she only had four to six months to live. It was time for her to make some hard decisions for the sake of her boy. She left the hospital feeling numb, even though Bernie held onto her arm. She cried for herself in the arms of this man she'd met at the Lexus Company a few months after she was hired. Each year, they'd become closer friends. Bernie was gay and lived with his partner. He cared deeply for Aaliyah and was a father figure for Lance. Bernie stayed with Lance whenever his mother had overnights in the hospital.

After several days, Aaliyah was amazed at the strength God had given to her upon request to put her business in order. She found peace with the fate she had been dealt, also upon request, she had made the decision she thought would be best for Lance when she was gone. One thing she was proud of was that, when Lance was born, she had a half a million dollar life insurance policy and a trust fund in place for his education throughout his childhood and as an adult. She wanted the very best for him. Bernie and his partner agreed that Bernie would take the role as father for Lance.

Dr. Hampton's father was the pastor of the church of which she'd belonged since she was a small child. In fact, her whole family attended. For months now, LaQuincy was in church every Sunday, helping out wherever needed. Her father was impressed with his eagerness to work and his energy. The members loved him and the single ladies eyed him, lustfully. Dr. Hampton had no worries and wore the rock to prove it. LaQuincy had retrieved all of his belongings that his family saved and stored in the city of Chicago. He sold a Michelangelo Buonarroti painting that he used to cherish. It had doubled in value and was now worth twenty-six thousand dollars. He made plans to sell them all. He wanted a total disconnect from his past. Pieces of expensive art now reminded him of his selfishness and amazingly, they meant nothing to him anymore. He bought Melanie a three carat princess diamond ring for $10,500.

LaQuincy loved his new life. Melanie would smile when he said he wondered what took him so long to get there to meet her, to understand the true love of a woman and to give himself to her and to God.

One Sunday, in his testimony, he said, "I now believe that when I became an adult, someone must've gathered up all the churches, along with my senses and hid them from me. There's no way I would've ever been out of church and out of touch with God had I known it was this good. I remember going to Sunday school and to church with my mother, but after I became a teenager, church and God became a distant memory. God is so good to me," he said. "He's good for keeping me all of those years when I was in the dark, living foolishly. Now I have this beautiful diva doctor who never gave up on me, who I honestly believe, God made just for me. I have this amazing church family, and I couldn't be happier. I'm just filled with gratitude that you all want to make me a deacon in your beautiful church. I feel so unworthy, but I do accept, thank you Jesus," he yelled, looking up, "and thanks to each of you," he said and sat down. Melanie reached over and kissed him.

After service each Sunday, LaQuincy went to AA meetings. He was now a counselor and a lead speaker for Sunday evening group. The group had multiplied since he'd become the speaker. The venue had changed three times to larger places and no matter where they went, they couldn't seem to accommodate the crowd. Eventually, the group was no longer associated with the name Alcoholics Anonymous because LaQuincy was talking a whole new language. Many of his church members joined him because he was so knowledgable teaching Bible principals, something many of the recovering alcoholics had never heard, and once they did, they were on fire for more, for Jesus, and they brought more people to hear Mr. Carpenter.

Chapter 26

Rudy and Diara grew further apart. He rose to the top of his career as she was fell deeper into depression. The accusations from Diara were more frequent and he had grown tired of being accused. He had done everything to prove to his wife that she was the only woman he loved, and he still loved her very much. He just couldn't convince her.

He joined colleagues, male and female, out for drinks after work one evening at the closest happy hour spot from the campus just to keep from going home. Diara wasn't so appealing in the state she was in, he thought. That was one of the things that had turned him off about Aaliyah. She was possessive and insecure. He liked a woman with confidence. Pilar Easley, a nurse and professor on campus had made it clear that she wanted Rudy for herself from day one, and told a female colleague that she was going to get him, if only for one night, but so far, he had not budged. She was a divorced, attractive blond who acted like she had rebottled youth. She was from a wealthy family in Denver, Colorado and was used to getting what she wanted. No one knew the details of her past in-depth, but it was rumored that she had been involved in a nasty divorce. That was what brought her to Hawaii, according to a coworker.

After a few drinks, she became very aggressive. She whispered in his ear, ran her fingers through his hair and rubbed his inner thigh under the table with her bare foot. He could've continued to resist, but his thoughts, like her behavior were altered by alcohol as well, which is also why by the end of the evening, he waited in his car for Pilar to join him. She had ridden to the bar with another professor, but made it clear that she would catch a ride back to her car on campus with Dr. Carpenter. They went back to his office on campus and before he could unlock the door, Pilar was all over him like an octopus, unfastening his pants and Rudy didn't stop her. They began to kiss, and in minutes, Rudy's desk was cleared and they were on it.

"What took you so long Dr. C.?" Pilar whispered.

"Trying to do the right thing," he answered.

"This doesn't feel right to you?" She asked.

"Oh yes, this feels great," he said. "Yes. It does," Pilar agreed.

"It's just like I imagined. You knew I wanted you, didn't you? I knew you'd be the most amazing lover," she said, while moaning louder and louder. "You're not so bad yourself girl," said Rudy. That's when his phone rang. He thought he should answer it but as he reached for it, Pilar pulled him closer, hoping to make it impossible for him to give his phone a second thought. And she did.

Diara called Rudy because he had never been this late getting home before. He always calls, she thought. Tonight, she had decided to greet her husband with something other than accusations. She had gone out earlier and bought some beautiful, expensive lingerie. Her hair was in big locks just the way Rudy liked it, and she knew the black and gold, 5-inch heeled pumps would do the trick. They hadn't made love in about three weeks and that was unusual. She thought she'd better get on her job because she knew her husband was in high demand. He was still exceptionally handsome with a gorgeous muscular body that was a definite eye catcher. He loved hot and spontaneous sex and she had not been the dutiful wife that he deserved lately, but all of that would change tonight, she thought, as she modeled and primped in front of the long length mirror. She checked on Christina, who slept peacefully in her bedroom. She lit two scented candles, poured herself a glass of chardonnay, and went into the kitchen where she had prepared a chocolate fruit tray that the two of them called their aphrodisiac. The table looked great and she felt great. She owed Rudy an apology, she thought. How could she have doubted her husband? "Just come on home baby," she said. "I promise to make it up to you."

As Rudy headed to his car, Pilar called out to him while lightly trotting toward him.

"Hey you, let me put something in your phone. What should I call myself, His Hottie?" She asked, smiling while pressing in her phone number and looking up at Rudy seductively. She slowly handed his phone back to him, kissed his cheek and they got in their cars and headed home.

"I don't know what I'm going to say to Diara," he said out loud. "I've never been this late before. Man that was stupid. I should've never let that happen. "

As late as it was when she heard his car pull into the garage, Diara was willing to excuse him because she felt that it had been her nagging that made him go out for the drinks she smelled on him when he walked in the door. There was nothing wrong with a night out with his colleagues once in awhile. He deserved it, she thought.

"Hi Sweetheart, come on in. I know where you've been and I'm not upset. I don't blame you. You deserve something different every now and then. I hope you enjoyed it, because I'm going to give you something that you'll enjoy as well. You just wait right here," she said.

Feeling beads of sweat on his face, chest and armpits, Rudy was speechless and a little nervous as his wife left the room. Guilt trapped his tongue and he couldn't speak, but if he could, he felt like this might be a good time to beg for his life. How could she know what I did? he thought, unless she followed me. Before the next thought could enter his mind, Diara stood before him, unrobed in a silk gold teddy, as beautiful as ever, with curls bouncing as she walked toward him. He had clearly misunderstood. His sexy wife wanted to make up, and he couldn't give her what she desired.

For the next hour, she tried everything to entice her husband. She poured him a glass of wine, fed him chocolate strawberries and danced for him. He seemed to enjoy it all, but when she got close to him, he stopped her, saying, "Hold on a second, baby. Let me take a quick shower and I'll be right back with you."

"No," said Diara, "you don't have time for a shower. I want you now." It wasn't until she helped him out of his shirt, not only noticing that it was drenched in sweat, but sure that she also smelled perfumeon it. She ignored it, but when she unfastened his belt, the scent of a woman's femininity met her nose. Now she understood why he hadn't responded. Disappointment quicklybrought tears to her eyes. .

"You bastard," she said quietly and ran to her room.

"Diara, baby please, let's talk."

Chapter 27

Like a father, Bernie comforted Lance at his mother's memorial service and carried him to the limousine in his arms. Aaliyah's family was there. Her mother had spent the last month with Aaliyah, caring for her and Lance. TaMar wanted to respect her daughter's requests, but she could not understand why she had chosen a gay white man to father her son, and why was he was so adamant about carrying out her daughter's wishes? Aaliyah's mother had chosen not to burden her with questions because of the condition she was in, but she needed more information. Bernie seemed to be rushing the family out of town. He had voluntarily driven family members to the airport and so did his partner. They hung around Aaliyah's house like they were hiding something, and with every trip they took to the airport, TaMar searched the house for important documents. She was determined not to leave until she unlocked the secret of this stranger who claimed to love her grandson like he was his own.

LaQuincy stood in the front of the church, close to the pulpit, waiting for his bride. His palms were moist. He was nervous, not because he was unsure, but because this was a dream come true. He and Melanie chose no best man or maids of honor. Just the two of them and their pastor, her father; who would lead them in saying their vows before God. Pastor Hampton smiled as his daughter was escorted in by his eldest son. Mrs. Hampton winked at her husband and they both smiled proudly. They were pleased that their daughter was marrying the man of her dreams. They were very fond of him, as well. LaQuincy's parents, sisters and nephews had flown in for the wedding. They had been there for the last couple of days, and were showered with kindness from Melanie's family.

The church was full, standing room only. The new member roster had grown in such masses because of LaQuincy's evening services; they were in need of another minister. Pastor Hampton chose LaQuincy and trained him for the task. His ordination would be the day after the wedding during the church service. He would become a salaried minister, counseling couples, helping individuals learn the Word of God. His parents were in awe of the life their son had attained.

LaQuincy read his vows, "Melanie Hampton, the woman who saved my life. I am so amazed at your grace, your beauty, your intellect, but most of all, your honesty and your goodness. You're everything that I wasn't. I never thought God would ever smile on me, but today, He's given me favor. I feel Him. He chose me. This is where I belong. You see," he said, turning to the audience, "I was a drifter, even when I thought I had it all, I was just drifting. Then I chose your name from a list of therapists because my grandmother's name was Melanie, and how significant that became. Yea, I never told you that did I? I needed help and God sent Melanie, like He did all those years ago, when my grandma Melanie would save me from whippings and pick me up from school when I pretended to be sick, right Ma," he said laughing. "But this Melanie is the one that I've been waiting for. She loves to please people, but I get a kick out of pleasing her. She has these facial expressions that I've studied, the one she's wearing now says, just wait until tonight, right babe?" The guests all laughed as Melanie lightly hit LaQuincy, blushing. "No, seriously," he said, "I'm going to spend the rest of my life delighting in your joy. I want to make sure your heart is full of happiness every day. I couldn't love you more if I tried. You're the blessing I never thought I would get. I'm so grateful,"

Melanie fought back tears to keep her make-up intact. Then she read her vows. "God is so amazing. He brings people together at the right times. This man has the most beautiful qualities of anyone I've ever known. I live to look into his eyes. He makes me feel like Super Woman. For the first time, I know what it's like to really be loved by a man, and he's right, I can't wait for tonight," she said and the audience laughed again. "I adore you my love. God has smiled on me today and given me favor. I feel Him. He chose me. I am so grateful." After a short pause, the pastor said, "Repeat after me."

The wedding reception was exquisite. It was held in the church fellowship hall, a huge elegant ballroom with gold custom made drapes, off white velvet, tall back chairs, flowing fountains, filled with Sparkling Cider. The cream colored, multitier cake accented with pearls spread wide and just as tall on a huge round table covered with gold tablecloths. Each large round table was labeled with ten guests' names and their meal choices, dressed in satin gold cloths and covered with silver, glasses and china to accommodate a four-course meal. After much mingling and dancing, families dispersed and the evening ended by 8:00. Everyone looked forward to the ordination the following day.

Chapter 28

"Aaliyah didn't know what she was doing," her mother told Bernie. "She would have never left that kind of a responsibility in strangers' hands. I found out why the two of you feel so strongly about keeping my grandson."

"Look TaMar, I'm doing what your daughter asked of me. She must've felt that I would take better care of Lance than anyone else would. She asked me and I was honored to do it. Your daughter and I have been great friends for the last five years. I loved her and I love Lance. I don't know why you question that," Bernie said.

"I think you know all too well," said TaMar, "Let me ask you something Bernie. How do you plan to support him? Did my daughter leave anything, like life insurance, anything?"

"Yes, she left him some money from a small policy," he admitted reluctantly.

"How small are we talking, a half a million dollars small?" TaMar asked. Bernie looked shocked.

"You…," said Daniel, gesturing to slap TaMar.

"No Daniel," yelled Bernie.

"Go ahead Daniel, make my day. You're both showing your true colors. Yes, I found a copy of the papers and my son is waiting in the other room for me to call him if you try anything. You thought you had gotten rid of everybody, but no, he's here and he will break you in half if I so much as say his name. Now I want my grandson to go back home with me. He needs his family," she said.

"That's not going to happen," said Bernie.

"I figured you'd say that," said TaMar. "So now I have to go to plan B," she said.

"No, we have to go to court," said Bernie, walking out the door with Daniel behind him. "I'll be back for my son in the morning," he said.

Pilar had been to Rudy's office nearly every day for a quick fix and he happily obliged her. They played the your office or mine game, sometimes twice a day. Diara was slowly unraveling. She had shut down, just going from one day to the next, doing nothing special. She volunteered at Christina's school a couple of days a week and that gave her some fulfillment, but other than that, she and Rudy were like strangers. He was out of control. He hadn't become abusive to her like LaQuincy had . He just ignored her. His late nights at work kept getting later. He once came home looking like he woke up to come home only to get ready for work. Diara had moved into another bedroom in the house. Therefore, some nights she didn't know what time he made it home. He was always gone when she got up each morning. They used to share a cup of coffee and he would take Christina to school. These days, it was obvious that he wanted to be somewhere else.

Pilar referred to him as her boy toy. She let him know early on, just what she wanted from him. "I don't plan to get involved emotionally with anyone, so don't give your girl such a hard time on my account, okay?" She said.

"Don't worry about my girl, okay. We're just fine," he said.

Her doorbell rang again and again. When she finally got to it, she saw Rudy through the window. She snatched open her door. "Why are you here on a Sunday?" She asked, standing in the doorway of her beachfront penthouse, half-naked. "You couldn't wait to see me at work tomorrow?" She said.

"You know why I'm here. Now let's get to it." he said, obviously annoyed, aggressively snatching off her sheer robe because of her unwelcoming attitude.

"Excuse me," she said, snatching her robe from his clutches, "No, if you must know. I'm getting to it with someone else today, so you need to leave and don't ever show up here without calling."

Rudy left angrily. He got into his convertible and broke every speed limit there was getting back home. Christina was in church with a friend and her family. Diara was home alone when Rudy walked into the house. As soon as he saw her, they started to kiss. Diara began to cry. She didn't know why her husband wanted her at this moment, and she didn't care. She was just glad that he did. They made love, but her husband handled her differently than ever before, as if he was trying to teach her someone else's ways.

"She rejected you, didn't she?" Diara asked. "I'm no fool Rudy," she said as she rolled out of bed. He just turned his back without a reply and went to sleep.

In a couple of hours, he was awakened by his cell phone. It was his sister Jackie. "Rudy, you have to come to Chicago. Mother's had a heart attack," she said.

"What? Why?" He asked.

"We're here because Quin's wedding was yesterday and today he was ordained to preach. He gave a testimony about something none of us knew about and Mother passed out. Just come, ASAP! And bring your family," she yelled and hung up the phone. He jumped out of bed. "Diara," he shouted.

"Yes, what is it?" she asked, running toward his voice, startled. "Jackie called," he said. "My family is in Chicago this weekend and my mother has had a heart attack. Get Christina. We need to get to the airport right away."

"Oh my, I'm so sorry, honey. Really I am," Diara said. "Do you need me to get some things together for you?"

"Yea, that would be great. I need to put things in place and find a sub for my class, and I'm supposed to assist in several procedures this week with some other doctors. Well, I'll make my calls and get some last minute reservations while you're doing that," he said.

LaQuincy paced the floor, outside of the Intensive Care Unit at the hospital. "LaQuincy, why did you tell?" Krissy asked. "We promised. You made me promise never to tell," she said.

"I had to tell Krissy. It was the only way I could be freed from it. It has ruined my life and I'm ready to live now. I can't hold on to secrets anymore. I'm sorry. It wasn't our mother's fault," he said.

"No, it was mine. I did this to both of you," said Sam, and he broke down and began to cry profusely. LaQuincy reached out to hug his father. "I'm so sorry son. I never meant to hurt you, or Krissy. Please, please forgive me, both of you, please." Sam begged.

"I do forgive you Dad," said LaQuincy, wiping his tears away.

"So do I," cried Krissy.

"Let's go to the chapel and pray. She's got to be alright," said Sam, "or I'll never forgive myself."

Melanie walked into the hallway from the waiting room and grabbed LaQuincy's hand.

"This is a mess, isn't it baby?" LaQuincy asked, sighing, while clutching the sides of his head.

It would be late Monday night before Rudy could see his mother. His mind raced and he barely felt when Diara squeezed his hand during the landing. What in the world could his brother have said to make his mother go into cardiac arrest? I'll kill him, thought Rudy.

They'd made it to Georgiaand only had a while before he could get to Chicago Memorial Hospital. As soon as they got off of the plane in Atlanta for a forty-minute layover, a random security check called for the Carpenter family to step aside. The family was frisked by officers and their bags were searched. One officer asked to see Rudy and Diara's driver's license. After retrieving them, he walked away. Upon his return, approximately 15 minutes later, he was holding handcuffs, walking toward Diara.

"Mrs. Diara Carpenter," said the officer, "you're under arrest for the kidnapping of a one Christina Carpenter."

"What? Are you serious? This is my daughter. No, No! Rudy, help," she screamed, struggling to get out of the officer's grip while they pulled her arms back to cuff her. Rudy yelled at the officers, begging them to listen. Christina was hysterical.

"This is my wife," he said. "And this is our daughter. Please listen, please!" yelled Rudy. "There must be some mistake. Let her go man."

"No sir, I'm afraid we can't do that," said the officer. "There's a warrant for her arrest, but you can come to the downtown precinct and try to get this thing straightened out," he said.

"LaQuincy did this," said Rudy, "Damn him," he yelled as he watched the officers walk Diara through the airport.

Chapter 29

TaMar had finally found Lance's birth certificate and Aaliyah's address book. "Mrs. Carpenter," she said. "No, this is her daughter, Krissy Carpenter. This is her phone, but my mother is in the hospital."

"Oh. I'm sorry; I was trying to reach her. I'm sorry she's not doing well," she said.

"I'm calling because my daughter, Aaliyah Sanchez, God rest her soul, has a son with your brother."

"A son? I remember Aaliyah. My brother brought her home for Thanksgiving once. And why did you say rest her soul? Is she…"

"Yes my daughter died from liver disease a week ago," said TaMar.

"Oh my, I'm so sorry to hear that," said Krissy. "Does my brother know about Aaliyah, or his son?" Krissy asked.

"No, I'm sure he doesn't. That's why I'm calling," said TaMar. "My daughter has left another man to father her son, and he's not a good man. He has wrong intentions. I know how much she loved your brother and I know he comes from a good family. I really hope that he will do right by my grandson. I have no legal rights, but your brother does. This man is determined to shut Aaliyah's family out of her son's life. Something has to be done, and quickly. He's taking him from me tomorrow morning." She began to cry. "I don't know what to do. I can't leave him with this man."

"Let me try to reach my brother. One of us will call you back ASAP, okay? Please don't cry. I believe my brother will definitely want to do the right thing for his son."

"Yes, thank you," TaMar said.

"Let me be sure I have your phone number," said Krissy.

Krissy walked out of the room where her mother slept peacefully. She saw LaQuincy and Melanie coming toward her.

"Quin, can I speak with you for a minute please?" Krissy asked.

Melanie went in to sit with Dee while LaQuincy and Krissy talked in the waiting area down the hall. Sam had gone back to the chapel. He went to thank God for the news they'd received about Dee's heart. The doctors called it a mild heart attack. She was scheduled for an angioplasty procedure. "She will heal well with lots of rest and a proper diet," the doctor told them. Dee vaguely remembered why she fell unconscious, and they all agreed to keep it that way. Nobody wanted her stressed.

When she saw her daughter-in- law, she whispered something to her that made Melanie's day. "I love you already. You don't know what you've done for my son. He's been through so much. You're just what he needed. I've never seen him happier. Thank you for loving him." "I've never been happier," said Melanie, hugging Dee carefully, and before she could speak another word, LaQuincy stood at the door, gesturing for her to step outside. Krissy smiled as she passed Melanie going back in the room to visit with her mother.

LaQuincy and Melanie went into the waiting area to talk. "I know you're probably going to think you should've married a normal man. Just when you thought you knew all of my drama, there's more. Just when I thought I knew all of my drama. But there's something I haven't told you. It's not because I was being dishonest. It's just that it was in the past and there was no need, but…"

Rudy had gone to the Atlanta downtown precinct to pay Diara's bail. He rented a car to drive to Chicago from there. He didn't want a repeat of what happened in Atlanta, flying into Chicago. Diara cried nearly the whole way. Christina asked Diara a dozen questions, beginning with "Mom why would someone say you kidnapped me?"

"I don't know baby," said Diara. After so many questions, Rudy told Christina that they would talk about it later. He felt horrible for Diara and she feared the danger ahead, the inevitable explosion between two brothers.

Rudy held his wife's hand and comforted her, even while his mind flashed thoughts of Pilar. He hated missing her touch, especially after she had the nerve to have someone else in her bed. How dare her, he thought.

Chapter 30

"Momma, Daddy, I need to talk to you," Melanie yelled running into her parents' house.

"Girl, what happened? Why are you crying?" Her mother asked.

"Please have a seat," she said. "LaQuincy has gone to New York. He just found out that he has a five-year-old son. A Spanish lady called his sister today to tell them that her daughter, the boy's mom died and someone else is trying to raise him, but for the wrong reasons. She wants LaQuincy to exercise his rights as a father and get custody of his son."

"Well, how do you feel about this, daughter?" Her father asked. "I'm thrilled Daddy. I get to be a mother," said Melanie.

"I couldn't be happier. I thought it would never happen."

"Well I've heard you say before God many times that you wanted Him to send a child for you to love. You trusted that He would do it, didn't you?" said the Pastor.

"Yes, of course, but ...," said Melanie. "Mel, it's not that I'm not happy for you dear," said her mother, "I just don't want you to get overloaded".

"How does LaQuincy plan to support his family? The church doesn't pay very much. You should not have to take care of him and his son," she said.

"Sweetheart, Sweetheart, calm down," Pastor Hampton said to his wife. "God will work it out. What I want to know is why he didn't know about the child," her father asked. "It's a long story, but I'll tell it if you have time. We don't have any secrets. I trust my husband."

"You know, you just said the magic words. If you trust your husband, then that's good enough for me. We have come to love LaQuincy, right Mimi?" Melanie's mother nodded yes in agreement, "and I trust him to take care of my daughter," said Pastor Hampton. "It is none of our business why this or why that about your household as long as you're happy."

"Thanks Daddy," Melanie said, hugging her parents, with tears in her eyes. "And Mom, don't worry. I'm sure you'll love the little boy too."

"I'm sure I will too Sweetheart. Forgive me for the skepticism."

At the hospital, after spending hours at Dee's bedside, Rudy walked to the cafeteria. "Rudy, where's Christina and Diara?" Krissy said as she ran to catch up with Rudy.

"They're in the room with mother. Why?" he says.

"I need to talk to you about a phone call I got yesterday.

Did you know that Aaliyah was pregnant with your son?" Krissy asked.

"What?" he says. "No, that's not possible. Aaliyah moved to New York years ago," says Rudy.

"That's not all," said Krissy. "Aaliyah died over a week ago."

"What? How?" Rudy questioned. "From liver disease," answered Krissy. "Oh my goodness," he said, stunned.

"LaQuincy went to New York to find out more about the boy," said Krissy.

"LaQuincy?" Rudy asked angrily.

"Why in the hell would he do that?" "Trying to help you, I guess. I didn't ask," she said, shrugging her shoulders.

"Help me? I don't think so, but I've had enough of him being so helpful here lately. That's it," said Rudy.

"Hello, it's nice to meet you. This is my son Tobias," said TaMar, shaking LaQuincy's hand. "Come in and have a seat. I'm sort of confused. Your name is on the birth certificate, but my daughter was dating this guy," she said, showing a picture of Rudy.

"Yes, that's my brother. It's a long story," said LaQuincy.

"Well, I have time and I want to hear it," said TaMar, "How do you like your coffee?" LaQuincy smiled and said, "Black please."

"Your mother can go home today. The procedure was a success and the sooner she gets home, the sooner she can begin healing," the doctor said to Jackie. "These papers will explain everything it takes for that process to begin. Take care of her," he said, turning toward Dee. "It's been a pleasure Mrs.

Carpenter. Take care of yourself and please do take it easy," said the doctor, smiling. She shook his hand and returned the smile. Everyone agreed. Sam had changed the reservations and they would return to Boston in a few days.

"Diara," said Jackie, walking out of Dee's room after hearing the news of her mom going home.

"Can I talk to you for a minute please?" "About what?" intervened Rudy.

"I said Diara, not Rudy," said Jackie.

"Well, again I said about what? But what I should've said was no, you may not speak to my wife about anything. In fact, stay away from her."

"Rudy, I don't mind talking to Jackie. I'm sure she has questions and some things she wants to get off her chest," said Diara.

"It's none of her business D," he said.

"That's ok Rudy, but you know you're wrong," said Jackie.

"That's why you don't want to talk about it." Rudy walked away quickly, holding Diara's hand.

"Remember," Jackie yelled, "God don't bless no mess."

Christina and her cousins were back at the hotel with Krissy. Christina enjoyed getting to know the boys, even though they were a few years older. She especially liked hanging out with her Aunt Krissy, her namesake. They had done each other's hair, played in make-up, and ate sub sandwiches with potato chips. Aunt Krissy thought the world of her niece.

"You are just a sweetheart Christina. I so love us hanging out like this. Maybe your parents will let you come back this summer to stay with me for a while. You'll get to spend time with Grandma Dee and Poppa Sam, Aunt Jackie and your cousins. It'll be fun. Would you like that?" Krissy asked.

"I would love that," said Christina, with a huge smile, hugging Aunt Krissy for the mere suggestion.

Chapter 31

"Can you do something to stop that kid from crying? I'm sick of it." Daniel said to Bernie.

"He misses his mother. She was all he had," said Bernie.

"I understand that, but he's calling for his grandmother," said Daniel.

"He'll get over it soon. What choice does he have? He belongs to us now," said Bernie. "I wish we could leave now, but we have to wait to collect the money his mom left."

"I know," said Daniel. "I just don't want anything to get in our way. This is a dream come true. We can finally have the things we've always wanted. After we get the money, we can ditch the kid, right? I mean like foster care or something like that." said Daniel.

"No, we're not ditching the kid. I promised his mother I would take care of him and that's what I'm going to do," said Bernie, sternly.

"The hell you are," yelled Daniel. "Listen to that little whiny brat. He hasn't stopped crying since you got him here. What's more important to you, what some dead woman wants or what your life partner wants? It's a simple answer Bern, honey. I mean, didn't sign on for raising someone's kid. It's too much responsibility." Before Bernie could reply, Daniel touched his lips with one finger, as if to silence him and said, "I'm going out for a run. Just give it some thought. Let's not let this thing ruin us. We never discussed kids. I had no idea you were actually considering this, my gosh. I thought you knew what the plan had to be from the start," he said, as he put on his jacket and walked out of the door.

Bernie stood still and shook his head, and then walked in the guest room to comfort Lance, who cried continuously, looking out of the window. "Hey little Buddy," he said to Lance, "come over and talk to me."

After TaMar listened to LaQuincy's story in detail about his short-lived sexcapade with her daughter, Aaliyah, followed by his apology, she showed him the birth certificate where he was named father of Lance Quincy Sanchez. Questions began to bombard LaQuincy's mind. Mixed emotions flooded his thoughts. Although he dared not say it aloud, he suddenly realized how real the situation was. He wondered if he could financially fit a child into his life and whether or not it was fair to ask Melanie, his new wife to take on such a responsibility. Would she agree to help raise a child neither of them knew? Could he be a good father to the child? He stared at the boy's picture that sat on an end table. He was amazed at the resemblance. There was hardly a question about him being a Carpenter. LaQuincy took a picture of the picture and sent it to Melanie.

Finally he spoke, "What exactly did you call me here for? What is it you hope to accomplish?" he asked.

"Do you want the boy for yourself or?" "I would love to have my grandson come home with me," TaMar quickly replied, "but I have no rights and if you don't fight for him, his future could be at stake. You are his father. He's five years old. Could you really walk away and let two strange, gay men raise your son? If you see him and you really don't want him, then help me to get him, please."

After taking a deep breath, LaQuincy said, "I need to speak with my wife. I will be back in a couple of hours."

"In the meantime, I will call Bernie Foley to bring Lance over," said TaMar, walking LaQuincy to the door.

"Ma, what do you think he'll do?" asked Tobias after TaMar closed the door behind LaQuincy. "I notice you didn't mention the money."

"I think this man has character," said TaMar, "but I want to be sure. I believe that Lance is such a great kid, that his father will want do the right thing, and either way, the boy will be with family." TaMar went into the closest bedroom and kneeled in prayer.

"So, now that you've had time to think, are we on one accord, now Bern? I mean, can we both agree to give up the boy."

"Yes Daniel. I love you enough to give up the boy," said Bernie.

"There's no way we can raise a kid. We both have to want the same things."

Daniel gave a sigh of relief. "Great, finally! Now I'm a little tired from my run, so I'm going into the shower and then take a quick nap," said Daniel, turning on the water for his shower.

"Fine," yelled Bernie. "I'm taking Lance to his grandmother."

"Yeah, that's a great idea," said Daniel, pulling towels from the linen closet. "Let him spend time with them while he can. He may never see them again after this week, and that'll be best for us."

"How's that best for us Daniel?" Bernie asked. "Well, because if we give him to them, then they'll want the money his mother left for us to raise him on, so it's best for him to go with strangers, you know, like foster parents, who know nothing about the money," explained Daniel, standing at the bathroom door, with only his face in Bernie's view.

"You have it all figured out, don't you?" Bernie said.

"Don't I always?" said Daniel, smiling, closing the door to the bathroom. Bernie sadly picked up the suitcases that were near the front door and walked downstairs with Lance in front of him. "Be careful little buddy, and put on your seatbelt," he said, while helping Lance into the car.

LaQuincy rang the bell to Aaliyah's house. Before the door was opened wide enough, LaQuincy's warm smile told TaMar before he could utter a word that he wanted to be a father to his son.

"Hello again, please come in and tell me, Mr. Carpenter, what's the verdict?" she asked, closing the door as they walked toward the family room.

"My wife is thrilled and she wants him with all her heart. She thinks it would be a good idea for me to stay here for a few more days so that he can get comfortable with me and we can put some legal stuff in motion as well. So, what's the next step? When do I see my son?" He asked with excitement.

TaMar's answer was interrupted by the sound of the doorbell. "Get the door son," she yelled.

Tobias opened the door to an excited little boy to see his uncle. Lance ran into the house, yelling, "Abuela, Bernie brought me back to you." TaMar and LaQuincy came rushing out.

"I know sweetheart," she said. "I asked Bernie to bring you over."

"No," Bernie said, "He's right. I'm really giving him back. He's been through enough. His happiness is very important to me. I do love this kid, no matter what anyone thinks," he said, bringing in Lance's things.

"Well thank you. Thank God," she said becoming teary eyed, looking toward the ceiling. "I am so glad you made that decision," TaMar said, retrieving a stack of stapled documents from Bernie's hands.

"I would like for you to meet Lance's father. The men shook hands while Lance stood in awe of the man introduced as his father. LaQuincy noticed the puzzled, yet happy look and kneeled before the child.

"Hello Lance," he said. "I am LaQuincy Carpenter."

"You're my padre', my dad?" Lance asked.

"Yes, I am," answered LaQuincy. "Wow," said Lance with a huge smile. "I never had a real dad before," he said. The adults smiled.

"Can I have a hug Buddy? I'm going to be leaving now," Bernie said.

Lance ran into Bernie's arms. "I love you Buddy," said Bernie.

"I love you more. That's what my mom used to say to me," said Lance.

As Bernie carefully placed Lance onto the floor, he rushed to the front door in a hurry to hide the tears that were hanging on the edge of his eyes. "Bernie," TaMar called as she walked toward him. "I misjudged you. My daughter did see a great man in you. I know she'd be pleased with the decision you made for her son today. I can't thank you enough. May God bless you," she said shaking his hand.

Chapter 32

Months later, Dee was on her feet again, but taking it easy. She and Sam prayed daily for their family to heal. Each morning they rose, they prayed for the blood of Jesus to cover each of their children and grandchildren. Christina visited for the summer as Krissy had planned. LaQuincy and Melanie had brought Lance to meet his grandparents and other family members. LaQuincy loved seeing Christina and had dropped charges against Diara for kidnapping the child. He felt that in order for his life to be blessed, he had to forgive Rudy and Diara. No matter what anyone said, he would always think of her as his daughter, he told Melanie. He'd loved her from the day she was born. He saw some of his features in her and the same ones in Lance, but that could all be family genes, he thought, since she was really Rudy's daughter. LaQuincy was very impressed with the pre-teen. She spoke four languages, fluently, from traveling with her parents. She was not afraid to hold a conversation with anyone. Before they parted ways, Christina expressed that she adored her Uncle LaQuincy and Aunt Melanie, and of course, the feelings were mutual.

Dee and Sam loved having all of their grandchildren near them. Sam especially enjoyed teaching Lance how to build things with harmless materials from his shed. Moreover, Dee discovered a precocious, adorable granddaughter in

Christina. She described the summer as one of the best she could remember.

Rudy continued his sex fling with Pilar upon return from Chicago. The entire campus was aware of the affair. His feelings for Pilar were stronger than he cared to admit. It was now known by his colleagues and the students alike that he would go into a jealous rage with other men for even conversing with Pilar. His superior was beginning to have concerns about Rudy's behavior lately. He was behind on all of the mandated initiatives required by the college. Others had been put on notice that Rudy's job duties suffered because of his extramarital activities.

Pilar, on the other hand had begun to enjoy the attention. After he insisted, Pilar told Rudy all about the person who was in her bed the day she rejected him. He thought it was one of the other professors. Eventually she introduced him to that person. Her name was Trudy. He wasn't completely satisfied until Pilar and Trudy invited him to join them for a ménage trois.

While Christina spent time in Boston, Rudy spent many nights at Pilar's penthouse, sometimes with Trudy, and sometimes without, but without so much as a phone call to Diara, who dressed in large clothing to hide the fact that she was five months pregnant with Rudy's baby. He had no idea because he had not touched his wife in months. Since they rarely talked, he didn't know that she had been diagnosed with clinical depression and slept sometimes more than twelve hours a day.

When school started, Christina woke herself up, fixed her own breakfast and caught a ride with a friend and her mother. When she came home most evenings, she'd check to see if her mother had eaten. Now and then, she could talk Diara into taking walks with her. She knew her mother wasn't well and she became her caregiver.

LaQuincy and Melanie had fallen in love with Lance and vice versa. Lance was happy for the most part, except for those times that he was reminded of his mother for some reason. However, his new mother, being a psychologist, knew just what to do to help him through his crisis. She loved him like her own and so did her entire family. "Lance is easy to love. He's handsome, mannerable, smart, very smart, and talented as well, just like his daddy," she'd say to anyone who listened.

LaQuincy continued his ministry on Sundays and the congregation continued to grow by leaps and bounds because of it. He had peace and never complained. He wanted to be able to help Melanie more financially. In fact, he wanted to shower her with gifts, vacations, and every great thing possible, but he was content with the beautiful life God had bestowed upon him and he knew that if God so desired, he could allow him to do more. She never complained. He thought of her like a dream come true and Lance as a gift, both from God.

One afternoon, when Melanie got home from work, she snatched the mail from the mailbox only to see another bill that quickly reminded her how much the bills exceeded their incomes. Her appointment book wasn't as full as it had been a year ago. The recession had made people put their shrink at the bottom of their priority list.

She walked inside and realized by the silence that she was home alone. She sat on the couch, placed the mail in her lap, kicked her feet up on the coffee table, laid her head back and let out a loud sigh, followed by the words, "Help us Jesus."

Before the first tear fell, her mother's voice rang out, "It's happening, isn't it?"

"What Mom? What are you talking about?" she asked, raising her head.

"You're overloaded just like I told you, aren't you? Business isn't so great and you still have to pay most of the bills around here," her mother said. "Do you need help? Dad and I can help you, honey. Don't hesitate to ask. I knew this would happen. You know I love LaQuincy and Lance, but it's hard for me to see my successful daughter taking care of a man and his,"

"Watch it Mom," Melanie said quickly. "Lance is my son and he and his daddy mean the world to me. In fact, Mom, they are my world. If money is the only problem we ever have, then we will surely be alright. God has provided thus far, and He will continue," she said, watching her mother pace the floor. Melanie was becoming more and more agitated with her mother's "I told you so" attitude. She was thinking, I don't know why I didn't lock my door when I got in this house. She tuned her mother out and fingered through the mail on her lap. Bill, bill, bill, umph, wonder what this is from Arrington Insurance, she thought as she tore open the large envelope and pulled out a stack of papers. A puzzled look came over her face, and she rose from the couch, looking at the unfolded papers harder. "Ma, Ma," she said, trying to get her mother's attention with her hand, but to no avail. Mrs. Hampton rambled on continuously about her daughter's financial woes, "Ma," she yelled, never taking her eyes off the papers in her hand.

"What?" Her mother yelled back, startled.

"Look at this," Melanie said, giving the papers to her mother. "Does this say pay to the order of LaQuincy Carpenter, $500,000?" Melanie asked pointing to the words on the paper.

"Oh, Sweet Jesus, yes!" her mother said.

They grabbed hands and began to jump around on the floor, squealing and laughing like they had hit the lottery. When they calmed down, they read the entire packet and were glad that Aaliyah had made such a huge effort to ensure her son a great life.

Melanie called LaQuincy and asked him to pick up Lance from school and come home right away. She had a wonderful surprise for them both. LaQuincy completed the sermon he planned to deliver the following Sunday. However, he was slightly delayed because of a bit of confusion about the title of the sermon. After only seconds, he smiled, as if God had handed it to him from the Heavens above. He then said it and wrote it with total satisfaction, "The Steps of a Good Man." He placed it in his desk drawer and followed his wife's request.

Chapter 33

Sam and Dee hadn't had their entire family home in years. There had been so much strife between Rudy and LaQuincy, Dee was beginning to think things would never be the same. She had been praying for years about the situation and it seemed to get worse all the time.

"Could this thing between the boys be irreparable?" She asked Sam.

"What you're really asking," said Sam, "is if this situation is too hard for God. Then, the answer is no. Nothing is too hard for God. We are true testaments of that. I thought you would never forgive me, but God is always working things out on our behalves, even when we can't see it and it looks like nothing's changing. Do you think our prayers are in vain? And if you do, then why do you insist on us praying together every morning?"

She laughed and said, "You are my rock, Sam Carpenter, you know that? Whenever I lose my perspective, you always have a way of pulling me back in, making me see things with my spiritual eye and not just the naked eye. Come here you big lug," she says, grabbing him around his neck to kiss him.

"God can work things out with our sons and He will, won't He?" she said. "It's already done," said Sam.

"Carpenter has misplaced important materials for the research project, and the presentation is today at 2:00," said Dr. Tattleson. "And he's been very nonchalant about it," he continued.

"Yes, I'm aware of his lackadaisical behavior these days," said Dr. Yim. "He's been written up at least twice in the last year." After a moment of silence, Dr. Yim said, "That's sad to see a man risk it all when he was the best at his work when he first got here. His research was thorough and his presentations left his cohorts unsure of themselves," said Dr. Yim.

"He hasn't even been here the last few days," said Tattleson, "but then again, Nurse Easley is missing as well."

"No surprise there," said Dr. Yim, "but if he doesn't show up today, that's it for him. He's been warned."

Rudy was just getting dressed to go home to prepare for a presentation that he'd not even thought about when Diara called. Lately he had begun to feel guilty about the way he was treating his wife. They not only shared a beautiful daughter, he thought, but the situation that brought them together should have been enough to keep them together.

"What is it, D?" he asked answering the phone.

"I need you to come home right away."

"I will but what's wrong Sweetheart, you don't sound too good?" he asked, sitting up erect.

Suddenly Pilar recognized kindness in his voice toward his wife and a jealous streak appeared that Rudy had only just begun to see whenever Trudy came around.

"Don't you dare talk to her in my house. What in the hell is wrong with you?" She said pushing him.

"Stop," he said in a whisper, while beginning to fill a bag with his belongings.

"No, I won't stop. You practically live here and now you want to be disrespectful to us both. It's not going to happen. She may be stupid enough to deal with it, but I will not allow some cheater to try to start back cheating with his wife on me," she said.

Rudy tried walking away from Pilar, but she followed his every step, screaming and cursing. He could hear Diara crying. He knew it was because she could hear Pilar yelling in his ear.

"Get away from me. I won't be cheating with my wife on you. I should've never cheated on my wife with you. Now leave me alone. I'm out of here, for good. I'm sick of this madness," he said.

Suddenly, he felt all the hurt and pain he'd caused Diara. He wanted to take her in his arms and apologize for all of the ugly he had brought to her life. He hated hearing her cry. He realized at that moment how much he loved his wife. That had never changed and from today forward, he would make it up to her, he thought. He knew it was he, who had stolen her joy, and broken her spirit. That saddened him greatly. Finally, Pilar had stopped shouting and left the room.

"I need you to come home now. It's an emergency." Diara screamed.

"Oh, my God, Baby, tell me what's wrong. I'm on my way," he said, worried about the urgency in her voice. "Sit tight," he said, running toward the door with his bag.

However, before he made it through the door, a huge hunter's knife penetrated his stomach with a force that was indescribable. He saw an evil Pilar holding the handle that was slowly being covered with blood, until he felt his sight fading, along with his strength and hit the floor. Diara gasped in fear. She stood in shock, hoping she was wrong about the sound she heard from Rudy, and then the sound of his body falling to the floor. She had no idea where he was or who the woman was that he was with.

Contractions were closer now. She called an ambulance. She didn't want to take a chance on the baby coming with no one there to help her and while she waited, she contacted Chandler's mother to pick up Christina from school. She tried telling the ambulance drivers about her husband but they didn't have enough information to go on and her labor pains had become so excruciating, that she was nearly delirious.

"Lord, don't let him die. God, please just don't let him die," she repeated over and over in a whispery voice. Then hard labor pains took over, and once Diara heard the medical tech say the baby was in distress, by no choice of her own, Rudy became a dim thought in Diara's mind.

LaQuincy and Melanie's lives were constantly changing for the better. Melanie purchased a building that she remodeled and turned into an art gallery to surprise her husband. LaQuincy's expensive pieces of art displayed beautifully. She had persuaded him to keep them after the sale of the Michelangelo. She knew that one day, it would benefit them, but she had no idea to what extent. She had each piece appraised and discovered a piece by Leonardo da Vinci worth over $900,000, a Vincent van Gogh worth $257,000. This man was worth a fortune, and he'd had no idea, thought Melanie, smiling and shaking her head.

LaQuincy was surprised and delighted that his wife had taken such an interest in something that brought him so much joy in the past. He realized through therapy that his love for art did not have to be erased from his past. It had been something that gave him peace when nothing else could. He and Melanie shared a love for art and took on a new venture to learn everything they could about the art world. Then they began to make connections to trade with and purchase art from some of the largest galleries in the United States, France and Europe. The work that he'd done earlier, photographing celebrities was also in the gallery. He was advised that he had to purchase the rights to all of his own work, and he did, with pleasure.

Christina pleaded with her friend Chandler's mother, Ms. Wallace, to take her to the hospital to see her mother. She wanted to know if she'd had the baby, and she wanted to be sure her mom was not alone. Christina knew her parents hadn't been getting along so great lately, so she wanted to be there for Diara, who had already been alone for hours.

When they arrived at the hospital, they went to labor and delivery, and found Diara's room. She'd had the baby and was napping in recovery. She had been given an emergency c-section because the baby's pressure had began to drop so drastically. A friendly nurse led the way to the nursery to let Christina see her baby brother.

"He's beautiful," said Christina. "My mother said if it was a boy, she would name him Rubin, and a girl would be Ruby."

"Those are very nice names, Christina," said Mrs. Wallace. "Well girls, I think we should allow your mother some time to rest and we'll call and check on her shortly. And, if she's up for company, I'll be glad to bring you back, okay?" She said to Christina.

"Yes ma'm, thank you," said Christina, politely.

"Your baby brother is so cute," said Chandler.

"He's just adorable," said Mrs. Wallace.

"I hope I can help you take care of him sometimes," said Chandler as they continued to look at the baby through the window of the nursery.

"Sure you can. I would like that."

As Christina, Chandler and Mrs. Wallace headed out of labor and delivery, they ended up walking through the emergency room.

"We must've taken a wrong turn," said Mrs. Wallace. "Stop here girls. I need to ask where the parking lot is for labor and delivery. I don't know how we ended up in here."

They heard over the PA system that there was a stab wounded man on the way to the hospital by ambulance. While the girls waited for Mrs. Wallace, they heard, "African American male, approximately 35 years old, unconscious, losing blood, stabbed in lower stomach, pressure rising." In seconds, EMTs were busting through the double doors. Chandler spotted the man on the stretcher.

"Christina," said Chandler, in a panic, "Isn't that your dad?"

Christina turned around and saw that it was Rudy, but in an instant, he was wheeled out of sight.

"Mrs. Wallace, that was my dad," she said.

Mrs. Wallace turned to Christina and asked, "Are you sure honey?"

"Yes Mom, she's sure. I saw him first," said Chandler.

"I have to see him. I can't just leave him. He's hurt. Did you hear all the things they said about him on the intercom? Please Mrs. Wallace, tell someone I need to see my dad," she cried.

Nearly two hours had passed since Mrs. Wallace explained to a lady in the triage area that Christina's dad had just been brought in. Finally, one of the doctors came out to talk to Christina and explained to her that her father had lost a lot of blood and because he had a rare blood type, they wanted to know if she was willing to help her dad if possible. Without hesitation, Christina jumped at the chance to help.

"Yes," she said, "What can I do?"

"Well sweetheart, we would do what we call a type and cross to see if your blood is a match for your dad's and we'll go from there," said Dr. Douglass.

"Follow this nice lady and she'll get you ready, okay?"

Chapter 34

Pilar went to teach her 2:00 class as usual. She had showered, changed, and stepped right over Rudy who lay outside her penthouse where she pushed him after he fell. She seemed to have had no remorse for stabbing him. She left him to die. After her class, she went into her office and closed the door.

"They won't know it was me," she said as she paced the floor. "They'll just think he was robbed or something. Anyway, he had no business talking to her at my house. The cheating bastard. First, he chooses Trudy over me, now his wife. What did he think? It's just like I told Derrick. I will never play second to ANYONE," she screamed.

Interrupting her, an intern knocked on Pilar's office door. "Professor Easley, Are you alright?" He asked.

"Yes, I'm fine, why?" She said.

"Dr. Yim and Dr. Tattleson would like to see you in Dr. Yim's office."

"About what?" She asked.

"I don't know ma'm. I'm just the messenger," said the intern, walking away.

When Pilar walked into Dr. Yim's office, she was asked to have a seat. She could feel an interrogation brewing.

"What's this about? I was about to leave for the day," she said.

"Have you seen Dr. Carpenter? I know the two of you spend a lot of time together," said Dr. Tattleson.

"No, I haven't. Why?" She answered.

"Let's just cut to the chase Professor Easley. We have reason to believe that you and Dr. Carpenter are intimately involved," said Dr.Yim.

"Oh really, and where did you get that reason?"

"From the obvious, but that's beside the point. The thing is," said Dr. Yim, "he's been neglecting his duties lately and he missed an important presentation this afternoon and we thought maybe you knew where he might be."

"No, I have no idea where he might be. Have you called his house, or spoken to his wife?"

"Well, of course we have, but we didn't get an answer. Now don't deny that you and Dr. Carpenter haven't been the hottest thing going on this campus. In fact, I would say that your relationship is now considered old news," he said, smiling sarcastically.

"First of all, it's none of your business who I get involved with, but for the record, Dr. Carpenter and I haven't been *involved* for some time now, so if there's nothing else, I do need to get home. Good day gentlemen."

Both men stood while Pilar passed them, leaving the sweet scent of her favorite fragrance in their noses. "I don't believe that for a minute," said Dr. Yim.

When Diara awakened, a nurse was wheeling in her baby.

"Hello Mom," said the nurse, as she lifted him out of the bassinet. "I brought someone to see you."

"Oh my goodness," she said, taking the baby from the nurse. "Hello baby. You are so beautiful, just like your sister. You are just perfect. I can't wait for your daddy to see you. Speaking of that, has there been any word on my husband?" Diara asked.

The nurse looked puzzled. "Earlier, I told another nurse about my husband missing, or possibly being brought in to the hospital because of an accident," noticing the puzzled look of the nurse, she said, "Just forget it. I just need to make some calls. I'll figure it out later, thank you," Diara said.

"Sweetheart, why are you crying?" Mrs. Wallace asked Christina.

"My blood wasn't a match for my dad's. So now, he has to wait for a donor."

"It's okay. You just need to pray for your dad. He'll get a donor. Just watch and see," Mrs. Wallace assured the child, as she held her in her arms. "We'll check on him again tomorrow sweetie," she said, "Let's go so you can get some rest. We'll come back early tomorrow morning."

"To see my Mom and Dad?" Christina asked. "And your baby brother," said Chandler. "Yes, and Rubin," said Christina.

Rudy lay in ICU, still unconscious, and sure enough, as Mrs. Wallace predicted, a donor was found. Hours later, Rudy had received a blood transfusion. When he started to wake up, he heard some unfamiliar voices.

"Looks like whoever did this was trying to kill him. His little daughter wanted so desperately to help him," a nurse said.

"Oh, you mean the little 12 year old girl?" said another nurse. "I think she must be his step daughter. We did a type and cross and he's not her father."

Rudy laid in bed wanting to speak, but couldn't. He felt the tears fall from his eyes and run down the sides of his head.

Oh my God! How can this be? This cannot be true, he thought, but DNA tests don't lie. Did D lie about this? No, she wouldn't lie about something this serious, he said to himself. The rest of the night, he laid awake thinking about all of the pain he had caused for so many of the people he loved. He tried to speak, but his voice was too weak to be heard. He couldn't move without aggravating an all too painful stomach wound. He hoped for a nurse to come and administer pain medication. They had to know he couldn't make it through the night without it, he thought, but they never came. While he laid in sheer agony, he began to talk to God about relieving him of the physical pain that was induced by his mistress. After only a short while, God did answer his prayer. The pain had nearly totally subsided, but the pain of knowing that

Christina was not his daughter would linger on forever. He then felt gratitude for his Father above and used his time wisely. He repented for his sins, even down to the beginning of his current demise; stealing his brother's wife. He prayed for restoration for his family. Before morning, Rudy felt that he could face the next day, whether good, bad, or indifferent. God had granted him peace, the kind his mother had always told him about.

Mrs. Wallace brought Christina back to the hospital bright and early the next day as promised, and she was the first face Rudy saw when he woke up. He had been moved from ICU to a private room. Christina smiled when her dad's eyes opened and he greeted her with a smile as well.

"Are you alright, Daddy? I was so worried about you."

"Yes baby, I'm alright, better than I've been in a long time. Were you here yesterday?" he said.

"Yes, and things didn't look well for you at all last night. I was so afraid to leave you.

What happened to you Dad?"

"That's what we would like to know, young lady. You mind if we have a word with your dad for a moment," said one of two officers, entering Rudy's room, and standing behind Christina.

"Dad," said Christina. "I'll go upstairs and visit Mom, but I'll be back soon."

"Mom?" Rudy asked.

"Why's your mom upstairs?" "She had the baby last night, silly," laughed Christina.

"Baby?" Rudy asked, confused.

"Mr. Carpenter, we just have a few questions and I promise we'll let you get back to your daughter," said the other officer.

"Okay, but Christina, please come right back," said Rudy.

"Hi Patrice," said Diara, calling the college for Rudy,

"This is Mrs. Carpenter. Has my husband been to the office this morning?" After a pause, Diara said, "He hasn't called or anything? That's not like him. I'm afraid something has happened. I probably need to talk to Dr. Yim. Maybe he knows something. Could you please transfer me to his office?

Chapter 35

"Say hello to Daddy, son," said Diara, as Christina pushedher into his room by wheelchair with the baby in her arms.

"D," said Rudy, "Oh my gosh baby. I had no idea. A boy? I have a son? He is just beautiful. Was he born full term? Why didn't I know you were pregnant? Wait don't answer that. I've been such a fool. Baby, I'm so sorry," he said, sitting upright on his bed to see the baby.

"Well, I do have some questions," said Diara. "What happened to you? Did this happen while I was talking to you yesterday?" She asked.

"As a matter of fact, it did, but let's talk about that later, please," he said. "I promise to tell you everything. Right now, I just want to hold my little boy. Is that okay?" Rudy asked.

"Sure," said Diara. "He needs to feel his daddy." "What's the little guy's name?" He asked Diara.

"I had planned to name him Rubin, but if it's alright with you, I really want to name him after my dad, Patrick, with your middle name, Patrick Nicholas Carpenter," said Diara.

"That is more than alright with me," said Rudy, gazing at the baby in his arms, smiling like a kid at Christmas. Christina beamed with hope and excitement as she watched her parents bond with their new addition.

LaQuincy and Pastor Hampton had just chosen the blueprint for the new church.

"I need to get home. Mel's doctor's appointment is later this afternoon. She thinks she has a virus, probably caught it from Lance's school. She's been doing a lot of volunteer work there. Lance is really doing well, except he's really worried about Mel. I think he's afraid that she will leave him like his mother did. Your daughter is a wonderful mother, you know."

"Oh, I know that, and pretty protective of him too, huh?" Pastor Hampton asked while getting into the passenger seat of LaQuincy's Escalade.

"You know it," said LaQuincy. After a few minutes of silence, LaQuincy looked over at Pastor Hampton and asked, "What's on your mind, Pastor?"

"You know Son; it's because of you that our congregation has grown to the place where we have to build a new church. Many years ago, when I started this church, I had big dreams of enlarging to the size of a mega church, like we have today. But I became content when we moved into an actual church from a storefront. Then I was even more amazed that we had to start an evening service to accommodate the new members, but we kept growing and now we have arrived, and I, well, I guess what I'm trying to say is that I have decided to appoint you Senior Pastor of St. James. I sure hope you accept it. I feel that you're the man for the job. I've been there, done that and I think the young families here need a young family to lead them. You, my daughter and Lance are just what this church needs," said Pastor Hampton.

"This is definitely an honor, but what about the older members, Pastor? They still need you," said LaQuincy.

"And I'll be there with you," said Pastor Hampton, "but you're moving this church in a way that motivates people, from the youngest to the oldest, even me and that's what we all need, someone who makes people excited about life. I know this is a lot to take in, and a huge responsibility. So go home and talk it over with Mel and let me know what you two decide."

"What about my mother-in-law? Does she know about this?" LaQuincy asked.

"Does she know? Son, she suggested it," Pastor Hampton said proudly.

When Pilar walked to her office from class, her phone rang. It was Trudy. Before long, the two were in a shouting match. Pilar waited until she locked her office door to really express herself.

"You had no freaking business at my house," she said. "Why did you go there? Were you two meeting while I was on campus in my classes? I knew you wanted him for yourself all along," she said. "I should have never introduced him to you. Where is he, Trudy? What hospital? Trust me; I'll deal with you later." After a couple of seconds, Pilar hung up the phone and talked to herself, as she dug into her purse, searching for her car keys, "I've got to get to that hospital," she said as she closed her office door to lock it. "I can't let him tell the police that it was me," she said.

"He already did," an officer said. "Pilar Easley, you're under arrest for the attempted murder of Dr. Rudy Carpenter. You have the right to remain silent..."

"No! I didn't do it. It was Trudy Wells," she yelled, wrestling to keep the handcuffs off.

"Settle down ma'm. Don't make this harder than it has to be."

"Oh my gosh. You have got to believe me. I did not do this," she screamed.

"Thanks for your help, Dr. Yim," the officer said.

"This is unfortunate," said Yim. "I knew there was a problem after speaking to Dr. Carpenter's wife this morning. I am so sorry it came to this. However, I'm not surprised about the fallout."

"Oh, shut up," Pilar yelled, as she was escorted down the hallway by two officers.

The doctor and a nurse walked back into the room after doing a thorough check on the patient.

"Mrs. Carpenter, you don't have a virus at all. You are about five weeks pregnant though. What you've been experiencing with nausea, vomiting and light headaches is morning sickness," said Dr.Lampley.

"Excuse me," said Melanie, in total shock.

"You must be mistaken. I can't have children," she said.

"Well the urine specimen and the blood test say otherwise. Maybe you need a moment to take it all in, but both tests are positive, and you can schedule an appointment with an OBGYN to confirm it, but it's definitely true," said the doctor. "Did someone come with you today, Mrs. Carpenter?" asked the nurse.

"Yes, my mother is in the waiting room," Melanie said quietly.

"Would you like for me to get her for you?" The nurse asked, smiling. "Yes, please," said Melanie, returning the smile.

Laughter filled the office as the nurses and doctors listened to the cheerful screams and squeals of Melanie and her mother after Melanie delivered the news that her mother would be a new grandmother. "Oh thank you, Jesus! My daughter can give us a baby. Let me call your dad," Mrs. Hampton said.

"No Mom, not yet." He's with LaQuincy and I want to tell my husband first, okay?" Melanie said.

"Sure baby!" said her mother. "I totally understand that. I'm just so excited." The two ladies hugged again and squealed all of the way out of the doors of the doctor's office.

Chapter 36

Dee and Sam were excited that Rudy and his family would be moving home soon. Rudy was taking a job as a physician in the Massachusetts General Hospital downtown Boston.

As his contract reached its end, Dr. Yim had recommended that Rudy not continue as Director of Medical Research because of all the embarrassing drama with Pilar.

"The media has ripped us a part behind this situation. Therefore, I feel that it would be in the best interest of the university for us to find a new director. We have some positions open as dean for some of the departments if you would like to look into those, but," said Dr. Yim.

"No thank you Sir. I'll be just fine."

All Dee knew is that she would have two more grandchildren that she could see on regular basis. She so looked forward to it. Also, their son, the doctor, could look out for her and Sam in their golden years, she thought. Sam hadn't been at his best lately and the doctors weren't able to pinpoint the reason for the pains he was feeling in his lower stomach and groin area. Sam had spent evenings in severe pain and after visits to the Emergency Room, he would take the pills that would ease the pain, but the problem, whatever it was, still remained. Dee hated watching her husband suffer. Rudy would be there in the next three weeks and maybe then, Sam could get some permanent relief.

Diara watched and enjoyed her four months old son. He gave her a reason to wake up in the mornings. He was simply adorable. She had begun to feel like herself again. She was getting out more, had become friends with some of the mothers of Christina's friends. She was finally enjoying Hawaii.

After watching the story of Rudy and Pilar on the news and finding out more sordid details than Rudy cared to offer, she decided to pick herself up and become a champion for her children. She hired a personal trainer to get back into physical shape and she and her daughter shared girl time at the salon, getting the works, weekly. Every day, she became more confident and Rudy admired his wife again, but from a distance. Their separate bedroom arrangements had not changed since they'd brought the baby home. After the media described the person, Trudy Wells, who rescued Rudy after the stabbing, as an additional sex partner to him and Pilar, disgusted, Diara felt that she needed time to decide if she would even stay with Rudy.

One evening, after Patrick's first birthday, as she and Christina were leaving the salon, a very handsome gentleman with an Australian accent came rushing out to the parking lot to stop her and said, touching her shoulder, "Excuse me, please.

Could I please have a moment of your time?" You're absolutely stunning and you are perfect for my project."

Smiling at the compliment, Diara says, "What type of project?"

"I am the founder of TayKenChancesWithLove Productions," he said pointing to the huge building behind him that read the name he'd called. "I'm looking for a leading lady for a new series. I know you've heard of the CSI shows. Well, this is CSI Hawaii. I don't want just anyone. That's not the way I do business. It has to be magical for me and you are the one I've been waiting for." He could see the reluctance in Diara's eyes and gestures. "Please," he said, "before you say no. Let me show you what I'm doing, and what I've done."

Christina smiled wide and nodded positively as Diara looked to her for a "should we?"

As they toured the building, they both saw huge poster- sized pictures of celebrities and shows that they had seen on TV, all produced by Liam Taylor, the founder and most pleasant tour guide. He showed Diara off to some of his employees who also agreed with Liam, that she was perfect for the part. "Take this card, and this contract. Look over them both and give me an answer tomorrow. I will be happy to make any adjustments you need," said Liam, smiling, while reaching for and kissing her hand. "Just please, please say yes."

Between LaQuincy, Mrs. Hampton and Lance, Melanie hardly had to lift a finger. The new church took up a lot of

LaQuincy's time, but he always made time for Lance and Melanie. He and Melanie made a promise that they would always put family first. Melanie handled most of the business for the art gallery from home and her mother helped her whenever she needed to go in. A couple from their church was hired to oversee the gallery until Melanie could come back full time.

Melanie was now five and a half months pregnant. She had surprised LaQuincy with that news months ago, and he called himself the most blessed man in the world. Today, he joined her for her doctor's appointment. They learned that they were having a girl, just what they'd both hoped for. The couple was astonished by God's goodness. They sat in the parking lot and talked after their doctor visit. "I told you Mel. God is smiling on me, and he has been from the first day I met you," said LaQuincy. "It's because of you baby, not me," said Melanie. "You're a wonderful man, Mr. Carpenter, and the best daddy ever. Our children are so blessed." "Mel, do you mind if I name our daughter?" LaQuincy asked. "No, I don't mind, as long as I can pronounce it," she said laughing. "Oh, it's simple," he said. "I want it to be Ruby. Ruby Nichole Carpenter." "Because of your brother, Rudy," she said, nodding in agreement. "I love it and I love you. You have just shown me why God smiles on you." They kissed and went home to celebrate their news with Lance.

Chapter 37

"So you will make a decision about our family and I have no say so. When did we start doing that?" Rudy asked. "Really Rudy. You don't want me to answer that do you?" "Please Diara, baby, don't do this. I thought we had decided to take it slow and try to work things out. My mother and father are expecting us all to be there this weekend, not just me. They haven't even seen the baby. Please D., think about what you're doing," begged Rudy. "I've taken a position at the General Hospital in Boston. I can't just tell those people I'm not relocating after all. But, maybe…" "No, Rudy. You should go to your parents. We've been discussing this for over a week now and I'm not leaving here. I have something new and exciting in my life now for the first time in heaven knows when. My children and I are going to stay here. If things change, or this doesn't work out for any reason, then we'll join you, but right now I'm preparing for a leading role in a series and I am all in. I know you understand what it means for your career to take precedence over what your spouse wants, right?" That's not fair, D," he said.

Tears wailed up in Rudy's eyes, as he began to understand that nothing he said could change Diara's mind. "Can I just take Patrick?" he asked. "No, you may not. My children are all I have," said Diara. "They stay with me. We will visit whenever we can. I'm not trying to keep them from you, but too much has happened. I am amazed about the way things changed for us. I thought we'd be in love forever," said Diara. "We still are, aren't we, D.?" Diara's phone rang. "Excuse me. I need to take this," she said holding out a finger to Rudy. "Hello," she said. In an instant, a smile covered her face that made Rudy remember when he was the cause of that smile, but he also knew that he had been the cause of her brokenness and depression, which is why he contained the anger he felt when he heard the sweetness in her voice as she spoke. "Yes Liam, of course I can be there," she said, raising her cell phone to put in the address for the GPS. After a short pause, she answered, "Really, you're sending a limousine? Wow, I guess I'm not dreaming after all. I am playing in the big leagues," she said as she laughed and walked out of the room for a more private conversation. After another pause, she said, "Oh, Christina is so excited. We saw the place yesterday. It's a dream, just absolutely perfect. Thank you!"

When Diara ended her conversation with Liam, Rudy went into the bedroom where she was. "D, can we talk? He said. "Sure, "she said, "but I have to be ready by 4. Liam is sending a limousine. Can you please pick up the kids?" She asked. "No problem," said Rudy. "We'll be recording the show for the first time on Tuesday," said Diara. "There's so much to do to get ready. I have some wardrobe changes and there are some suggestions I want to make. So I need to be on time. What do you want to talk about?" "Really, Liam's given you that kind of power already? I remember when you came in with Christina last week and said that he approached you leaving the salon. Do you think he has another agenda?" He asked, getting an aggravated look from Diara. "I didn't mean anything by that, sweetheart," he said, raising both hands. "I just thought that when you're hired in that business that everything is all scripted for you." "Well, he owns the studio and he created the show," said Diara. "So, he's accepting ideas from his team, and I'm just a part of that team," she explained.

Rudy sat at the foot of the bed and rested his elbows on his knees, his head dropping automatically to the palms of his hands. Losing his family was quickly becoming a reality. "God help me! Please," he said to himself. Diara started to undress to change for her appointment with Liam. She wrapped herself in a short red silk robe and pulled a white suit from the closet. She went into the bathroom to turn on the shower. When she came back into the room to put her accessories together, she noticed tears falling to the floor from Rudy's eyes. Her heart went out to him. She knew she still loved him, but she had been through hell, putting him and his career above her own life and Christina's. Therefore, she could not give in to his demands. He'd hurt her too bad. She walked to the bed and sat beside him. For a time, they sat in total silence. The room was still. Finally, she touched his shoulder and he leaned in to her arms and began to cry harder. Raising his head to look into her eyes, he asked, "Do you forgive me, D? I know all of this is my fault." "Of course I do Rudy, but it's not all your fault. I made mistakes as well. But yes, I forgive you. I love you." "Do you, baby?" Rudy asked, hopeful and surprised, as he wiped away his own tears.

Slowly, they started to kiss and Rudy's magical touch reappeared and like old times, Diara's body gave into it. She needed it and right now she craved it, from him only. No one could make her feel like Rudy could. His muscles were still as hard as ever, rippled, one hill at a time, like an Almond Joy candy bar. He was born for this thing called making love, she thought, as her hand traveled down his chest, gently rubbing his washboard like torso, and then running into the three-inch scar that another lover caused after realizing she would never feel his touch again.

The thought of the other woman made her cringe, and she wanted to make him stop kissing her neck and take his hands off of her, but who was she kidding? She knew she was at the point of no return. She understood how his violent lover felt. She never knew a woman Rudy had loved that didn't get shook up in a major way. One had relocated and drank herself to death, while another had tried to kill him and he nearly drove me crazy, she thought, as her body continued to follow Rudy's every physical command. "But ain't nothing like this," she declared in her mind, "and I mean absolutely nothing."

Thank you God. She still loves me. I can tell she missed me, Rudy thought to himself because of the response from

Diara. I don't know what I would do without her. How could I have been such a fool? She's still really the only woman I've ever loved. She's so beautiful, with the body of a goddess. I can't imagine another man's hands on her, he thought, looking at Diara as if he was touching her for the very first time. I haven't touched this woman in over a year, and she stayed. Talk about a lucky man. Let me stop getting it twisted. I'm not lucky. I'm blessed, he thought. The moans and groans of love rang out through the Carpenter house for old time's sake. Love was on their side again. "Baby, please say you love me," Rudy whispered.

"I do. You know I do," answered Diara softly.

Diara rushed out of the shower after their afternoon sex session because she heard the doorbell ring. Rudy had answered it and was about to send the driver away, but Diara stopped him just in time.

"What are doing, Rudy?" She asked irritated. "Please wait for me in the car. I won't be much longer," she said to the driver.

"Yes Madame, please take your time. Mr. Taylor is in no hurry," said the driver.

"Is Mr. Taylor in the car?" Rudy asked, although no answer was returned to him from the driver. He walked back to the car as if he was under strict instructions to only speak to Diara.

"Turning toward Rudy, perturbed, Diara said sternly, "I have an appointment at 5:00. You knew that. What is the problem?"

"Baby I thought we were going to…,"

"I'm not discussing this with you right now," said Diara, "I'm going to finish getting dressed. Can you please pick up the kids like you said you would?" Without answering, Rudy went angrily into the garage, got in his car and drove quickly past the limo.

Chapter 38

"Jackie, I need you to pick up Rudy, Diara and the kids from the airport tomorrow at 4:00 and make sure you have room in your car," Dee told Jackie. "I'm not sure if they have a car seat for the baby. I am so excited and I think your dad's even more excited than I am. I thought this day would never come."

"Yea Mama, I know, but David's going to pick up the golden boy and his family.

"What do you mean, golden boy? Are you still upset with your brother about Quincy, girl? Quincy has moved on with his life. He has Mel and little Lance and I told you last week that they're having a baby girl. He's about to be Senior Pastor of his church. Don't you know he would not want you to hold a grudge against your brother because of him? He's over it and you need to do the same," Dee said.

"I'm not holding a grudge, Ma, but what they did was wrong," said Jackie.

"Well, baby, if we cut everyone out of our lives for doing wrong then we'd all live alone. You have to forgive your brother. And the thing is he and Diara seem to be doing fine. Quin and Melanie are doing great. I don't know why they made the decisions they made and what led them to it, but I can't hold that against my son, or his wife. I am not their judge, and nor are you," said Dee.

"I know exactly what led them to it," said Jackie. "Quin trusted Rudy to escort his wife home because she was supposedly afraid of flying, which I find hard to believe, but he had a thing for her the first time he saw her in your kitchen."

"Maybe so Jackie, but all I know is that they chose to come here to raise their family. If you alienate them, then you alienate those two innocent children. So, Aunt Jackie, try thinking about picking your battles."

"Okay, Ma. Maybe you're right. I don't want any problems between Rudy and me. It's Diara I have the problem with," Jackie said.

"Well then, you still have a problem with your brother," said Dee.

"Those two are in love and we might as well get used to it. So let me get off this phone. I've got to check on your dad.

I'll talk to you tomorrow," said Dee.

"Bye Ma," said Jackie.

When Diara made it home from the meeting, everyone was asleep and she was anxious to get in bed herself, but she knew they'd be leaving the mansion in the next couple of days and there was so much packing to do. She went into baby Patrick's room and smiled as she spotted her baby sleeping peacefully. She finished packing up his things and went into Christina's room to do the same. Rudy woke up when he heard her stirring. He joined her and they quietly completed the packing of their belongings.

Chapter 39

The new church was huge. It could easily seat 15,000 people, which that number was fast approaching. It was said that once you heard Pastor Carpenter, there was no turning back. He had a way and a testimony that made people come to terms with their faults, and their strengths, gifts and talents. People's lives were changing right before each other's eyes. They were growing as individuals and collectively. It was obvious that God was present in this holy temple on Sundays, and doing a daily work in the lives of His people, with Pastor Carpenter as their shepherd.

While her daddy preached, one-year-old Ruby Nichole walked from pew to pew, grinning and babbling to members of the church. Melanie and the child's grandmother kept up with her as much as possible, while Lance attended children's church with many of his friends, some from school.

Dee was cooking dinner when Krissy walked through the door. "Hey Ma," she said, kissing her mother's cheek.

"Hey, what are you doing here?" Dee asked. "I came by to see Rudy. I have a friend who works at Massachusetts General and says she knows of an opening they have for a physician," said Krissy.

"Yea, well they probably wouldn't give it to him. He had the job, but because Diara and the kids didn't come home with him, he rejected the offer thinking she would let him stay with them, but she didn't, so the position was filled by the time he got here," Dee explained.

Jackie opened the door and walked inside her mother's house. "Hey you two, what's going on?" She asked.

"I was just trying to help Rudy get a position at MGH, but Ma says he blew it," said Krissy.

"Yea," said Jackie, "I'm afraid she's right. He claims he didn't know Diara and the kids weren't coming until the last minute, and I think she's just one cold hearted witch to do that to him," said Jackie.

"I mean, my goodness, hasn't she hurt enough people in this family?"

"Well, being that this woman has played such a major role in both of my sons' lives, I wanted to know too, why she wasn't coming with her husband. As far as I knew, this was a decision they had made together. I wasn't totally satisfied with her answer because of the kids being separated from their dad. However, what I didn't know was that my son took Diara through some pretty ugly stuff. A woman that Rudy had an affair with stabbed him and left him for dead while he was talking to Diara on the phone, the same day she had the baby, and she didn't know where he was or what to tell police. And what's even crazier than that is that Rudy had no idea that his wife was even pregnant," said Dee.

"What?" Chimed in Krissy and Jackie.

"Were they separated?" Krissy asked. "I don't know, apparently so, or maybe he just wasn't paying attention. You know how some men do. When they are into someone new, they may never look at you again. But, to finish what I was saying, Diara was on antidepressants and poor Christina was left alone to fend for herself."

"Aww, that's so sad. That poor baby had to go through that all by herself," Krissy said, nodding her head. "Where is Rudy now?" She asked.

"He's where he is every day, in his favorite spot, out there in that dreadful shed with some old buddies as he calls them, drinking their lives away. I wish I'd done away with that shed years ago. It was key in taking a toll on this family. I hate it, but I guess this was inevitable," declared Dee with tears in her eyes.

"Looks like Rudy has brought us full circle," said Krissy.

"Yea, in his father's sins," Jackie said, walking over to hug Dee, and the two of them joined by Krissy.

Diara was thriving. The show was a hit and the cast had just recently learned that they were up for an Emmy Award and received the news of another season for their hit series, CSI Hawaii. The kids were in private school. Liam was still as attentive as he had been from the day they met. He did whatever Diara asked of him, and she knew she was being overpaid and wouldn't think of complaining about that, therefore she saved a lot of money for what she called , "a rainy day." She was beginning to realize that Rudy was right about Liam's agenda. He finally said to her that he had given her ample time to get Rudy out of her system, and was thinking they could take their relationship to another level. As far as she knew, they only had a working relationship and little did he know, getting Rudy out of her system would probably never happen. She still loved her husband but they just couldn't be together.

She had received a letter from Rudy months after he left, telling her that he was finally able to give her the space she needed and how he wished her a great life. He apologized over and over again for the hurt he'd caused her, and didn't blame her for choosing not to be with him. He hoped that one day she would allow his kids to come to Boston to spend time with him and the rest of their family, but no pressure. Finally, he ended the letter by telling her that he had never known love like hers before, nor had he ever loved like that, and he was looking for a reason to justify why he made the mistakes he'd made, but there wasn't one worth mentioning except for arrogance and foolishness, and how different things would be if he was ever given a second chance, but again, no pressure, he signed, "Yours for Life, R.C." Diara was weakened by his words, but held fast to the decision to continue the life she had made for her family.

Over the next two years, Rudy's drinking problem had spun out of control. He woke up drinking, and continued throughout the day. He was angry and unemployed. His money had run out and it was very difficult for anyone to have a civil conversation with him, even Diara, who even by phone, could see that things had drastically changed since he'd been gone.

Although Sam's chest tightened from the stress of the situation, he tried approaching Rudy once for getting out of line with Dee while in a drunken stupor and that opened up a huge confrontation. Rudy blamed Sam for the way he'd turned out, for the way he'd treated his wife and for his drinking habits. Sam was a man of faith these days and had been now for many years, and was unscathed by the accusations from his son, but he felt pity for him and he knew he needed help.

That was the day he placed the call that could lead to a new and improved life for Rudy or possibly more destruction, but it was a chance he had to take. His greatest hope was that love would conquer all and all parties involved would realize and believe that blood is thicker than water, and "when one of us is in trouble, no matter what's happened in the past, we must come together and pull him/her up by the bootstraps and hold on to them until they can stand strong again, because that's what families do," he said to a doubtful Dee.

"But Honey," she said to Sam, "there's just so much bad blood."

"Well, there's a baby named Ruby Nichole," said Sam, picking up the phone. "The name alone tells me that there has been some resolution and forgiveness."

The day before LaQuincy's departure, he stood at the altar alone in the church where he delivered God's word every Sunday, and some throughout the week. He thought about some of the toughest and most complicated assignments God had relinquished to him. He remembered being afraid of whether or not he could offer correct councel to couples in a way that would assist in the survival of their marriage, "but God, you saw me through," he said.

"There are numerous happy couples in our church that are witnesses to what you've allowed to take place using me as a vessel," said LaQuincy. "I've been in hospital rooms and in homes of people who had lost all hope and you've given me what was needed to even heal the sick, words to console broken hearts and the strength to guide this huge flock of people. But today God, I come to you as humbly as I know how. I beseech you in my next assignment more than ever. On tomorrow, I will face my greatest challenge yet, my brother.

Chapter 40

LaQuincy felt a bit overwhelmed as the flight touched down in Boston, his hometown. This visit would be different from any other. He was going to help a brother who had betrayed him in probably the worst way possible. Good memories ran through his mind of times when he was a kid who looked up to his big brother. He thought the sun rose and set on Rudy. After all, back then, his big brother was the only man who had not disappointed him.

Then his mind shifted to a more complicated time when he would've killed his brother on sight for the ultimate betrayal, but he was now a godly man. His mind and thoughts were disciplined. He had forgiven Rudy and his ex-wife, and he hoped that she'd forgiven him. He'd hated himself for a long time for what he had done to her. God had blessed him with such an amazing life; there was no room for unforgiveness or to begrudge anyone.

Melanie had wished him a successful trip. They'd prayed together before he left. Lance had jumped on his back, yelling, "Dad, I'll miss you," and Ruby told him to hurry back so he could go to church. He charged Lance to look out for the girls, which made the ten-year-old very happy. He shared butterfly kisses with his three-year-old daughter and ensured his wife that she was still the most beautiful creature that God had ever made, and he could hardly wait to be back in her arms again.

The reunion between Rudy and LaQuincy had been difficult and strained at first, which was somewhat expected, but on the third night, Rudy poured himself a drink and his heart out right behind it. Through tears, he begged his brother's forgiveness for stealing his wife. It had not been planned. He never wanted to hurt his brother that way, he said, but also, drunkenly, he admitted that she was just the most perfect being he had ever seen, "and I had to have her," he said.

"Don't forget about what you did to her, while you sit here so innocently, Mr. Man of the cloth," said Rudy.

LaQuincy caught himself as old feelings of hatred rushed back as he listened to arrogance spew from his brother's lips. He properly excused himself from the table before trouble took place in Dee's kitchen. Dee had filled him in on the ugly things Rudy had done to Diara as well, which was why his family was not with him.

Rudy continued to pour and drink Jack Daniels and hardly noticed that his brother never returned to the table. He was found face down at the dining room table the next morning by Dee and LaQuincy. When Dee woke him up, he walked right out to the shed in the backyard. Getting through to Rudy was going to be tougher than LaQuincy expected. His brother was worse off than LaQuincy was aware of, especially if he had resorted to using the *shed.*

Each night, the two men conversed and as usual, when negative emotions began to rise up and control him, LaQuincy quickly excused himself. By day six, there was no more talk of the past, or of Diara or Aaliyah. LaQuincy invited Rudy to an AA meeting. He wanted to help his brother get his life back, and get his family back. After sitting in the meeting for a few minutes, Rudy had excused himself to go to the restroom. After the meeting, LaQuincy found him standing beside the car, nearly drunk from a flask he'd secretly carried in his pocket, but he didn't give up on Rudy. Like Melanie saved him, he was determined to pay this debt forward, no matter what it took.

Each day afterwards, they went to a meeting somewhere in town. One evening, LaQuincy spoke to the crowd and gave his testimony, which stopped Rudy at the door, as he was about to leave. He had never known what had happened to his brother. It was hard to hear such devastation. He wished he could've protected his younger sister and brother from that horrific nightmare. Tears came to his eyes as he walked back to his seat, realizing that that was the story that led to Dee's heart attack. The tragedy that LaQuincy talked about had happened in her house and was kept secret, while wreaking havoc on one of her children year after year. Rudy listened to others' horror stories for the first time and his heart went out to them as well. They had all taken their families through hell. One of the women, who was an alcoholic, finished her testimony by looking directly into Rudy's eyes, or so he thought, saying words that would change his life. "Time is wasting in a bottle of many regrets. You're blessed if you get more than one chance to make your mark on this world."

The next few evenings were easier and welcoming from Rudy. He sat and listened each night until the night before LaQuincy left to return to his family. That was the night that Rudy gave his testimony. LaQuincy was disheartened by Rudy's troubles and wished him well. He felt that he had completed the task assigned to him by his father. However, before leaving his parents' home, he placed in Rudy's hand, an inscribed Bible. The inscription read, "*When You Can't, He Will. Nothing's too hard for God.*" The men hugged tightly and Jackie escorted her younger brother to the airport.

Later that night, and from that night forward, Rudy read from the Bible and attended meetings diligently. He called his brother from time to time when he had questions about a particular scripture. There were pictures of LaQuincy's family within the pages of Rudy's Bible. He cherished them. He saw a handsome boy who looked a lot like LaQuincy, with Aaliyah's eyes and wavy black hair,a prettylittle angel that was surprisingly his semi-namesake and a beautiful woman who smiled like marrying LaQuincy had made her Queen. It was obvious that they were a happy and wholesome family. This wasn't the first time he'd been proud of his brother, who was surely a man God could depend on, Rudy thought.

"You came through again my love," said Dee to Sam. "You said our sons would settle their differences. Not only did they settle them, but they're on the road to restoring the relationship they'd lost. Rudy finally, really knows God for himself, as do our other children and that speaks to my very soul about my King Jesus," she said.

"I know. It started out rough. I watched and listened and I wanted to step in because at times, I felt that I'd made a mistake in bringing my sons together," said Sam, "but I began to see the changes slowly unfolding, and I thank God for what He has done. It's like Sam Cooke said baby," as he slipped his arm around his wife's waist to dance and sing to her, "It's been a long, a long time coming, but I know a change gon' come." Dee squealed with laughter, followed by a howling of laughter from Sam as he dipped his wife.

Chapter 41

As Krissy added the finishing touches to the table, she smiled and said, "This anniversary party is going to be the best ever." Yes child, Dee and Sam are going to be so pleased. You all are some really good kids to do this for your parents," said Dee's sister, Sarah Bell.

"Well, Auntie, trust me, this is nothing compared to the ugly stuff we've put those two through, and I mean as adults," the two ladies laughed.

"Wow, I just can't believe that my sister has been married for 50 years, but I must say, they've come a long way. You know Krissy, I haven't always loved your dad, and I'm sure you've heard your mom say that our dad hated him, but if Daddy could see him now, he'd be well pleased," said Sarah Belle, smiling.

Everyone happily mingled, church members, family members and friends. A photographer made his way around the room taking candid shots of everyone. David searched the room for his wife, Jackie, while he wooed the crowd with his horn. He even asked Krissy if she'd seen Jackie. "Clearly she's not here," he said.

"There's no telling David. You can believe she's up to something, but you know she'll be here," she said, leaving David nodding his head.

Proudly, LaQuincy took charge of getting the crowd to take their seats before the honored guests arrived. Everyone laughed when his cute little four-year-old Ruby joined him at the podium, wearing a turquoise dress with ruffles, and hair in the cutest little bun. Melanie was just as pretty wearing a beautiful Vera Wane turquoise halter-top gown with streaks of brown throughout the dress to accent the brown Armani suit that LaQuincy wore with a turquoise handkerchief. The handsome couple complimented each other. Lance was just as handsome in his taupe colored suit with a shirt the exact color of his little sister's dress. Krissy wore a long black gown that hugged her petite body in all the right places, so an admirer from church thought anyway.

Rudy walked into the foyer area using his cell phone. LaQuincy saw him, stepped down from the stage, and walked to the door to greet his brother with a hug.

"Man, you're looking great, he said to Rudy, checking out his brother in a black tuxedo.

"Hey, thanks man, you're looking pretty spiffy there yourself," said Rudy.

"Come on over and say hello to my family. Where's your date?" He asked.

"I was just on the phone with her. She won't be able to make it. She sprained her ankle," answered Rudy.

"Ah, that's too bad," said LaQuincy.

"Well, not really. I've only seen her a couple of times. She's not really my type," he replied. After embracing his brother's family, Rudy and LaQuincy welcomed incoming guests while continuing to chat.

"Have you talked to your wife lately?"LaQuincy asked.

"Yea man, all the time. We're actually planning a visit from the kids in a few months. I'm looking forward to that," said Rudy.

"Any chance of you guys patching things up? LaQuincy asked.

"I doubt it. Don't get me wrong," said Rudy. "I would jump at the chance, but I think she's moved on."

"Well, I wouldn't be so sure about that, pointing to the door. There stood Diara in a flowing black gown with a red band around the waist. Rudy couldn't move.

"Still beautiful," he said. Both gentlemen were amazed at the teen that walked beside her mother, simply gorgeous, they thought. Before Rudy could ask how this all took place, in walked Jackie holding Patrick's hand.

"There's my son, man," Rudy said with pride.

"Quite a handsome little gentleman," said LaQuincy.

"Oh he got that from his dad," he said. The two men laughed and Rudy went to greet his family. LaQuincy looked on, happy for his brother and went to join his own family at the table.

Chapter 42

As the evening progressed, family members and friends honored Dee and Sam with words of admiration, respect and love, and gifts galore.

After the last person spoke, Dee said to Sam, "I think we should thank everyone, don't you?"

"Yep, let's do it," he said. She took his hand and asked why his palms were sweaty, but he shrugged his shoulders and said, "I'm a little nervous, I guess."

"But this is our family, sweetie," said Dee. "I know. I'm okay. Just go on and talk baby," Sam said, helping Dee to the podium.

She kissed his cheek before he went back to take his seat. She tested the microphone and said "Family, can I please have your attention?" After everyone quieted, Dee looked at her family and smiled a huge smile. "I can truly say that this is one of the most glorious days in my life. I stand here beside my husband and best friend, thanking each of you, as I fight back these tears that seem to keep popping up. I haven't always been able to say that my husband is my best friend, but today, I could shout it to the mountaintops. I am so proud of you, my love and the man that you've become," she said looking back at Sam, who smiled modestly. "I'm proud of each of you as well, our family and friends. My daughters know how to throw a party, don't they? They have my sister here from Dallas, Texas.

I love you Sarah Belle," she said, waving to her sister, "all of our grandchildren are here, and all of you. First, I want to say to my daughters, thanks ladies for being so precious in my life. They're my shopping buddies, my soap opera partners, and they just give me a life outside my home. They always include me in their lives and that's important for a mother. They take good care of their father too. He doesn't have to lift a finger when his daughters are around.

My sons, my boys have always made me very proud, but today, I am a living witness about what God can do. He repairs and restores lives and relationships. I'm just overwhelmed as I look out and see my sons with their beautiful families. I've imagined a day similar to this one many times that our family would be reunited. I'm just so full," she said. Sam helped Dee back to her seat, as she began to get teary eyed.

"My wife is right. This day is a blessing. Thanks so much for loving us enough to do this. I've imagined this day as well, but mostly I imagined myself saying to each of you to forgive me if I've ever hurt you in any way at any time. I love you all and I'm so proud of all of you, for all that you've come through and for whom you've become. Take ca…," Before Sam could utter another word, his eyes rolled upward and his facial expression changed; he clutched his chest and fell to the floor. "SAM," shouted Dee, rushing to the floor beside him.

Screams took over and a crowd quickly swarmed around Sam. Rudy was the first to get to his father, "Call 911, he said before begging the crowd to back away and allow Sam to get air. Rudy could see that Sam was unresponsive. He quickly began CPR, still nothing changed.

He tried again and again, and between his own tears and chest compressions, he realized something he did not want to accept, his father was gone, yet he couldn't give up. He cried hard and as he raised his head to look at the people who seemed to be holding their breath, waiting for good news, not a dry eye was in the house.

Dee shivered with fear. "Wake up Sam," she said. "Please don't leave me. I can't lose you now," cried Dee. Finally, the ambulance arrived and they worked hard to revive Sam, but to no avail. An EMT asked Rudy some routine questions, confirming what Dr. Carpenter had discovered about his father. They then loaded Sam into the ambulance and drove away, followed by a caravan of cars and SUVs. Everyone was devastated.

Chapter 43

Sam's death was the result of a massive heart attack. Rudy had been taking care of his father for the last six months, after accepting a job at Massachusetts General Hospital in cardiology, his favorite field of study. Bypass surgery was scheduled for Monday. Only Sam, Dee and Rudy were aware of the surgery. Sam should have stayed in the hospital, but he wouldn't hear of missing their anniversary party. Therefore, the three of them had planned to sit down with the rest of the family on Sunday evening to give them the news.

Instead, there was mourning about the absence of a man who had greatly impacted his family, influencing them to follow in his footsteps from his old habits in the days where sin remained his choice, until his life was nearly at stake. Then he was born again, and the day he died, he saw his family reunited, standing strong, acting on one accord, with Christianlike love for one another, just as God commands. That was his final request, and it was granted.

Diara had reached out to Rudy all week and the children enjoyed time with their father. He'd planned for a happier time to visit with his children because it was difficult to enjoy them in his time of grief. He could hardly believe that he would never see his father again. Only his mother and his siblings could relate to this heart breaking reality.

Dee tried to be strong for her family, but the fact is for the last few years she had reconnected with her husband and they together were better than they'd ever been. It was hard to let go. She was happy that he'd formed a close relationship with his children and had gotten the chance to see all of his grandchildren, but her heart ached to know that after the service today, that Sam would no longer make her laugh about becoming forgetful, or strengthen her when she was feeling low, or cook a small meal and light candles because he thought she was beautiful by candlelight. She chuckled at that thought, remembering telling Sam that he just didn't want to see her wrinkles. They'd both laugh and he would ensure her that she was wrong, that she would always be the beautiful girl he'd met when she was in his town on summer vacation, babysitting her aunt's young children.

Dee applied her make-up for the third time because of random tearful outbursts. Before leaving her bedroom, she sat on her bed, on Sam's side, touched his pillow gently and whispered, "I'll always love you, Sam Carpenter. You were my rock, ya' big lug." And she went to join her family in the limousine that awaited her.

After the last song was sang, the eulogy was eloquently delivered by Pastor LaQuincy Carpenter, Sam and Dee's youngest son. As he came to the end of his sermon, he said to his family, "My dad lived a long life, not as long as we would have liked, but his assignment here on earth was complete. He wanted his family to be together again. I guess you could say he sort of got his house in order, which, obviously can be done in more ways than just the one we all know of, which is to get saved and seek salvation. He desired restoration for us. We've been through many hard trials over the years, and we thought we would never make it to this point, but God is able to do what we think is the impossible.

"Now what I want to know is if there's anyone in my family who doesn't know God, but desires to know him. Will you take a stand today? I don't just mean family. I mean family, friends, and friends of friends, whatever. If you're here and you don't know Jesus, it's time. We all know Sam Carpenter wasn't always a man of God, but he had a desire to change and be saved. Now the only way that you can be sure to see him again is if you feel a need to change. Don't wait. Tomorrow isn't promised to any of us," said LaQuincy. "Come today. I promise you, God will change your life." He looked around the room and no one moved. "May God add a blessing to each of you," he said, and walked to his seat. Just as he sat in his chair in the pulpit, he suddenly heard a female yell out. "I do desire to be saved. I can't go another day. I want a change that only comes from the love of God. I've never as an adult had this opportunity and I will not go another day. I love the Lord, and I believe He died for my sins. I pray, but I want to be saved. I need Him for my children, for my marriage and for my life," Diara cried as she headed toward the podium where

LaQuincy now stood. Rudy picked up Patrick and took Christina's hand to meet their mother at the altar.

Shouting, crying and praising filled the entire church. Dee, Jackie and Krissy joined their family near Sam's casket and a host of other family members followed, either desiring prayer or to repeat the sinner's prayer. "My father is smiling down on this right now, family," said LaQuincy, loudly and cheerfully from the podium.

Melanie smiled as she watched her husband win the souls of his family for Christ.

Chapter 44

At the repass, the atmosphere was bittersweet; but, overall, the family was happy. Everyone reminisced about Sam and his homegoing celebration. "He would've been so proud today. The church was full of family and friends. Even Tainty Bogo got saved today," Krissy said laughing.

"Girl, who is Tainty Bogo?" Asked Aunt Sarah Belle, laughing, as well.

"Oh, that's one of my dad's old drinking buddies from back in the day," replied Krissy.

"I'm really missing my dad, but this has truly been a wonderful day. He has got to be smiling," said Jackie.

Later that evening, Rudy made a decision. He felt that he'd wrestled long enough with the fact that he had not been honest with LaQuincy or Diara about Christina's paternity. Now that he was a man of God, he wanted to do the right thing and make good decisions. He always felt that he owed his brother for the situation with Diara.

He hadn't said anything about what he'd learned at the hospital after his incident with Pilar. Out of selfishness, he tried to justify by telling himself that his brother was happy with his family and didn't need to know that Christina was really his child. Rudy couldn't bear the thought of Christina not really being his daughter. "They have to understand that it was hard for me to accept when I found out," he said out loud.

But today, he decided that he loved them all enough to tell them the truth. He'd tell the two adults and the three of them would decide the best time to tell Christina. He believed his dad's last words, "take ca...," was leading to telling his family to take care of each other, and this was where he planned to start.

He and Diara had been as close as ever since the night his father died. He'd partially blamed himself for not scheduling Sam's surgery sooner, and she'd consoled him and supported him like old times. She had reserved a hotel room, but canceled it after seeing the shape Rudy was in emotionally. They agreed that he needed his family with him at his place. He hoped they shared mutual feelings about reconciliation. She was on hiatus for the next three months and hadn't heard for sure whether the show was recommended for a new season this year. Therefore, she agreed to stay as long as he needed her.

Diara and the children got in the limousine with the family on the way back to Dee's house, while Rudy drove his car and stopped by his apartment after the funeral to change clothes and to rehearse. He figured the news about Christina would be quite a blow at first, but LaQuincy would be happier than anything to discover that Christina is his daughter. Either way, now was the time, he thought. No more secrets.

When he made it to Dee's house, he saw Diara opening a bottle of water for Patrick. He kissed the child and asked if he could talk to her outside in the backyard. She agreed, but was very curious.

Smiling, she asked, "What is this about? Are you okay, honey?"

"Yes, I'm fine. Just meet me out there in 5 minutes," he said.

"When he ran into LaQuincy, he and Melanie were looking for a room for Ruby to take a nap. "She's had a very long day," said Melanie in a very pleasant voice.

"Yes, she has," LaQuincy said.

"What's up Brother? You need to see me about something?" LaQuincy asked.

"Yea, actually I do," Rudy said nervously. "When you're finished here, could you come to the backyard for a minute?"

"Well, yea, of course. This sounds serious. Are you alright?" LaQuincy asked.

"I'm good," answered Rudy, walking away.

When Rudy saw LaQuincy come out of the bedroom, he dashed to the back door to beat him to the yard where Diara patiently waited. LaQuincy joined the two of them and felt somewhat awkward, but then Rudy began to speak.

"I called the two of you out of the house to meet me here because of something that needs to be said," said Rudy.

"Man, what is this all about? We've gotten passed all of this."

"He's right Rudy. What are you doing?" Diara asked.

"Okay, I won't beat around the bush," said Rudy.

"Christina's your daughter Quin, man," he said.

"What?" said Diara and LaQuincy.

"What are you talking about? Why would you say something like that?" Diara said, voice trembling. She began to cry, but muffled her mouth to listen.

LaQuincy said nothing, just looked on angrily, nostrils flaring, biting his bottom lip, waiting for an explanation. Rudy began to explain what he'd heard the night he was hospitalized and Christina tried to give him blood.

"Why are you just telling me this now? You've had plenty of time," LaQuincy said.. "How could you? Why didn't you say something?" Diara said, crying, as she reached in her pocket to check the caller ID on her ringing cell phone. She answered it and said, "Liam, I'm so glad you called. After a pause, she said, "Yes, the answer is yes," she said, staring at Rudy. "We'll be returning to Hawaii tomorrow." Before that news could penetrate Rudy's mind, LaQuincy drew back his fist and with all of his strength, punched Rudy in his face, knocking him to the ground and walked into the house. Diara stepped over him and followed LaQuincy inside.

The End

Stay tuned for Part 2

About the Author

Kellye B. Alston was born and raised in Earle, Arkansas, the fourth of five children to Tommy and Lois Davis. Kellye is married to her soul mate Patrick Alston from Norfolk, Virginia, who fully supports and shares her dreams. They have four beautiful daughters; Taylor, Kennedy, Chandler and Logan.

Kellye has been an elementary school teacher for nearly 15 years. She has a Master's degree in Educational Leadership/ Curriculum and Instruction and has at least 30 hours beyond that degree in Marriage and Family Counseling. She feels that the institution of marriage and family is God's greatest plan.

She and her husband are co-founders of their own production company called TayKenChancesW/Love Productions, named after their daughters. She has written at least nine stage plays that have been performed in her local community since 2001 under her direction.

Kellye hopes that her writing ministry will continue to enlighten, entertain and bring hope to people all over the world.